Beneath The Plastic

SD
ALLISON

BENEATH THE PLASTIC

2006

Beneath The Plastic

On *Momentum*, time accelerates to the point where faces and conscience blend into the backdrop of the unimportant. The present quickly falls into a forgotten past, making individual actions, for good or bad, lose all connection to each other, and all significance as a whole.

To a *Pretender*, the different characters played in everyday life are disassociated from each other, each unto themselves, completely separate from the Pretender's true self, which, if done properly, simply becomes another character. Each character, each part of that nonexistent whole, has free and individual will.

Charlie is a Pretender.

Charlie is on Momentum.

On Momentum, Charlie can pretend to be anything.

For Graham

CHAPTER 1

Charlie was sitting upright, underneath, as usual, pillows under his back, his head sunken into the satin, padded headboard. Mrs. Bernstein, his employer, was on top, sliding roughly up and down, her breasts bouncing and shaking, like hams in wet plastic sacks.

"Charlie," she whispers, "tell me I'm still beautiful."

But Charlie doesn't answer. Instead, he sits up as best he can, and pulls her close, burying his face between her D-cups. He grunts, and squeezes her back, and with her skin oozing through his fingers, the question is forgotten, just as it was last time, and all the times before that.

He tries to imagine, between breasts spidered with veins,

that he's somewhere else, doing this with someone else, but it's no use, and it never is. The old woman keeps talking.

"I could pass for forty, couldn't I, Charlie? The firmness," she pants, "they're too firm for a woman my age."

And Charlie just pounds away.

"Charlie," she gasps, a whisper in his ear, "you make me feel young again."

Charlie smiles to himself then, and picks up the tempo. She always gets sweet when she's about to climax.

Expectedly sudden, she grabs him tightly. He grunts a little louder. She moans a little deeper. He pounds a little harder, and she squeezes him tight between her thighs.

Just then, she starts to sort of whistle. Her dentures are losing their grip. Her tongue is jammed into them, trying to stifle her squeaks of orgasm.

Soon after, Charlie is in the bathroom hurriedly washing off the memories and rinsing the taste from his mouth. For Charlie, there's still cleaning to do, and seconds later, with dustwand in hand, and with all his precious muck still side-stroking in his sack, Charlie is in Mr. Bernstein's study.

Mr. Bernstein is Jewish.

Charlie has met people who think that all Jews are a part of a consortium bent on world domination through the manipulation and control of money.

These people are usually fun to be around.

He has also met people that think money is a carrot created by government to make us work and support "the system".

These people are fun sometimes as well.

They generally own firearms.

Mr. Bernstein owns a firearm, and, incidentally, also has a great deal of money.

Also of note, Mr. Bernstein, for the past handful of years,

has been confined to a wheelchair, and has not left the main floor of his home, and rarely leaves his study.

Charlie has never met anyone who has ever voiced any truly interesting opinions about wheelchairs, or those who use them.

"I'm sorry for the delay," Charlie said as he began to dust a bookcase.

"Yes, fine," Mr. Bernstein said, and eyed him over top the binding of the leather-bound volume in his hands. "That wife of mine runs you ragged, doesn't she?"

"Yes sir," Charlie said.

"Yes, indeed," he nods. "Busy, busy everyday, cleaning and scrubbing, cleaning and scrubbing."

"Yes sir," Charlie said again.

"Good then," he smiled. "She's getting my money's worth."

"Yes sir," Charlie smiled back.

A few seconds later, and right on time, Mrs. Bernstein comes hopping down the stairs and into the study.

She has on a tennis skirt, which strangely has never caught hold of everyday fashion like its partners the tennis shoe, and bracelet.

Or, maybe it has. I'm from Nebraska, and don't really know.

"My God," she groans, "it smells horrible in here! Charlie, do you ever bathe?"

"Yes ma'am," Charlie said.

"Well, you stink of something. God knows what."

"Easy on the boy, dear," Mr. Bernstein defends, his eyes fixed on his book, "he's the best we've had."

"I suppose," she huffs, and shoots Charlie a wink behind the old man's back.

Charlie fought off a cringe. It came out as a cough.

"But still," she continued, "if the boy we have in to clean, brings the stench of monkeys with him..."

"It's musk," Mr. Bernstein snaps and slams his lap. "Young men smell of musk. Charlie is a young man, and Charlie smells of musk. It's the scrotum, you know. That's the source. The testes. He's brewing mayonnaise for Christ's sake. You never knew me when I smelt of musk. You were nothing more than the scent of your father's loins, nothing more than mayonnaise yourself."

"Yes dear," Mrs. Bernstein shoots back, "and unfortunately your mayonnaise had turned to mold by the time we met."

"Perhaps," Mr. Bernstein said, "but my mayonnaise was not what you were interested in, was it, dear?"

"No dear," Mrs. Bernstein said, "I was only interested in love."

And everyone in the room smiled at this, because everyone in the room knew what sarcasm was.

What enticed Mrs. Bernstein, thirty years Mr. Bernstein's junior, to accept his proposal and become his second wife was, of course, the enormous fortune he inherited and added to. The former beauty queen was as shrewd as the man she married, but she did not expect him to still be alive, and in control of his fortune more than thirty years after their wedding.

"Well dear," Mr. Bernstein said, "I suppose you've planned a challenging day for yourself."

"Yes dear. I'm off to the tennis club now, and have a 3 o'clock massage."

"Don't exhaust yourself," Mr. Bernstein replied.

"Oh, I won't dear," she said, then bends to place a peck on his liver spotted head.

"Fine dear, careful then."

"Yes dear."

"Goodbye ma'am," Charlie said.

"You stink, Charlie," she said, and left the room, and the house.

"Amazing woman, my wife." Mr. Bernstein said once she was gone. "But she wears more lipstick than a drag queen. Please, Charlie, come here and wipe off my head."

CHAPTER 2

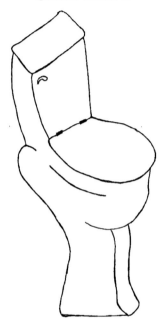

Charlie raced home from the bus. His bowels were losing their grip on lunch.

Cigarettes have two effects: cancer and regularity.

It's hard to run fast with your gluteus flexed shut.

Home for Charlie is his mother's apartment, further down the block. This is where Charlie lives.

There's nothing wrong with that.

The apartment was a typical one. It wasn't all that nice,

but it was certainly nice enough. It was much longer than it was wide, with the rooms branching off of a hallway that ran the entire length, from the front door to the bathroom. It had three small bedrooms, a kitchen, a family room and a coat closet by the front door. It was close to schools and public transportation.

It was a real one-of-a-kind, with thousands just like it.

Charlie calls his mother, 'Mother', like everybody else does, or would have, if there were anybody else around to do so. Rather, she always wanted to be the one that everybody called 'Mother', whether she was that person's mother or not. But no one comes around anymore, or really ever did, at least not with the sort of regularity that could give rise to a familiarity and closeness where one would endear a woman not related to them with the personage of 'mother'. It's ridiculous, nevertheless, this was her silly little dream.

There's nothing wrong with that.

But Charlie's mother, whom he calls, Mother, does not earn money for a living. She watches a lot of television and keeps many caged birds, and that keeps her happy enough.

Art once made her happy. Painting made her feel alive.

Paint dries over time, and becomes hard.

She did marry along the way, but the man Charlie called Father, had a heart attack and is now dead. Mother never had a job, and through her husband's death, she was promised to never need one.

Life insurance is a scam, until you die.

It's a sad but reasonably predictable fact of the family loins that Charlie won't make it past the age of 45. If he does, he'll have accomplished something his father, grand and great grandfathers did not. Charlie knows all this and accepts it with grace.

Carpe Diem is Latin.

Latin is dead.

Most Latin Americans speak Spanish.

But Charlie was about to soil himself on the steps of his mother's building, and that would be a horrible thing to happen to someone Charlie's age.

Inside the building now, and with the door to his mother's apartment in sight, Charlie fumbles his key chain of five keys hastily to get to the one he wants.

The door to the apartment has two locks, each requiring a separate key. He guesses then, it being the middle of the day, that only one of the locks is engaged, and upon jamming the key into the lock, and jamming himself into the door, Charlie realizes that he has guessed incorrectly, and inside the apartment, he hears the commotion he's caused.

Inserting another key, and entering the apartment, Charlie is greeted by the crescendo of coos, caws and the slapping of wings on the twenty odd birds that his ruckus has brought to frenzy.

"Lock the door, Charlie, lock the door, Charlie," Sajak said as Charlie danced like a penguin toward the bathroom amidst a downpour of feathers.

Sajak is a parrot, and the only member of the feathered bunch who can communicate in English.

Distinction.

Some argue that parrots aren't that bright, that they're only mimicking, only repeating things they've heard.

The same argument can be made for most people.

Charlie then trots past the family room and past his mother sitting on the couch in front of the television.

"How was class, Charlie?" His mother blurts out as Charlie blurts by.

"Fine, Mother." He said and rushed into the bathroom.

"Come tell me about it," she said, talking over the commercial, and the slamming of the bathroom door.

The dropping of corduroy and the relaxing of more muscles than Charlie can appreciate brings relief, and time to catch up on the world's events.

Charlie and his mother keep a newspaper in the bathroom. This was originally a quirk of Charlie's father, one that Charlie never fully appreciated until he became of the peculiar age where the event of a bowel movement becomes an opportunity to relax. And, oddly enough, this usually coincides with the age where the news inside the paper is something that becomes interesting, and something we feel we should know.

Pornography is another reading material often enjoyed in bathrooms.

Streaking down the drain and back to the world, Charlie joins his mother in the family room.

"Class was fine, Mother," Charlie said, answering again a question asked about ten minutes ago. And as he sinks into his father's chair, next to his mother's couch, he is greeted by cool, worn leather, and answered by silence.

Charlie notices that the television has concluded its paid advertisement, which was airing upon his entrance, and has rejoined the regularly scheduled program, which, at this time of the day, was Oprah, and there's no talking during Oprah. And, while we're at it, there is no talking during Regis. No conversation is allowed during The Price is Right, and none during The Young and the Restless. There's no talking during Days of our Lives, or As the World Turns. Nothing is to be said during General Hospital, and, of course, silence should be observed during Ellen, and that brings us back to Oprah. And as we've established, there's no talking during Oprah.

But Oprah doesn't last forever. Soon the news will be on, and Mother will idle for an hour and a half.

And when that time comes, Charlie's mother again asks, "How was class, Charlie?"

And to that, Charlie answered, "Just fine."

"That's good Charlie." Mother smiles.

"Have you eaten yet, Mother, or would you like me to make us something?"

"Something like soup would be very nice, Charlie. It's cold outside today, I've heard."

"You heard right. It is cold. Soup sounds like just the thing to warm us up. How about maybe we split a pot of tomato soup? How about maybe a couple of cheese sandwiches too, maybe to dip in our soup?"

"Oh, Charlie, you take such good care of me."

"Of course I do," he said without catching her eyes. "I'll get the soup on."

"Feed my birds, too, won't you, Charlie?"

"Of course I will," and of course he will, and of course he does.

CHAPTER 3

After the soup and the sandwich, and the update of all the juicy happenings of today's broadcast life, the world has spun to the point again where life picks up where it left off, and that's with Wheel of Fortune. And there's no talking during Wheel of Fortune, and there's no talking during Entertainment Tonight.

After that we're on to primetime, where Momentum again kicks in, making Mother's little Charlie something all together new.

After a change of clothes and on his way out, Mother said,

"I don't know how you do it Charlie, work and school. Your father would have been proud."

"Thank you, Mother," Charlie said, knowing damn well she hasn't a clue about anything.

And into Primetime Charlie goes, thinking not of the lie he's living with his Mother, fictitiously attending college and working nights to pay for it all, nor thinking of the adulterous prostituting of himself at the Bernstein's. With Momentum in his blood, Charlie has but one thought, the character he is about to become.

Charlie is a Pretender.

Charlie is on Momentum.

Charlie is running to catch the bus.

And he takes that bus only as far as he can, which isn't nearly far enough. He gets off downtown, quite some way from the warehouse he's headed for, and he'll have to walk it all. Charlie, right now, can't be seen on a bus.

Tonight, Charlie is homeless.

The homeless rarely use mass transit.

Stepping off the bus, and into winter, Charlie is bullrushed by a river of wind funneled down a canyon of glass, concrete and steel. It takes just seconds before he's cold to the bone.

The gloves he wears are as worn as his pants, which were once worn proudly by his father. His stocking cap is thick and warm, and a tight sweatshirt beneath a surplus army jacket does well with the cold and wind, but its all a waste with numb feet, face, hands and legs dropping his core temperature to a level that tickles his sanity.

And it takes about an hour to get to the warehouse, walking like a demon, but it wears him ragged and whips his cheeks ripe. He'll need that second bowl of soup he'll get when he arrives.

Walking along Jackson Street, the street he 'works', Charlie notices nothing new. No construction and no obstacles, nothing that would have interfered with his day, and more importantly, nothing specific that he might be asked about.

Conditions were poor today. The sun was bright, but it was too cold. The streets were empty. He only got a few bucks, never mind he wasn't there. The holidays are gone, and with them went the generosity. It'll be the same story the rest of the Brothers have been singing for weeks.

The Brotherhood of Panhandlers, of which Charlie is a member, and to which Charlie is heading for a meeting tonight, has seen better days.

Panhandling, as everyone knows, is a cyclical affair, much like the Fruit Cake and King Cake industries. The late autumn months, from Thanksgiving to Christmas, are the best time to be homeless, speaking strictly from a fiscal perspective. Spring and summer follow that. The income is not at the holiday levels, even with the increase in pedestrian traffic, but the weather is accommodating, which is certainly a perk of the profession. The time between New Year's and April, however, is just about unbearable, at least in this climate.

The homeless could stand to do without Black History Month.

And that time is now. Add that to a recent set of city initiatives to curtail panhandling and discourage the presence of the homeless downtown, and you've got little reason to wonder why the Brotherhood is in a state of strain, and flux.

Close to the warehouse now, Charlie begins to see faces he knows. It's time to cough and spit.

"Jackson," a man yells from across the street, and that man is yelling at Charlie.

He is Monroe Street, and he's been a very good friend to Charlie since the start, since they met outside the library several months ago. Monroe was in his forties, possibly his fifties, his body and face weathered to the point where an accurate guess was not possible. He was thin and gray. If he had money he would have looked distinguished, but he didn't have any, so he just looked like a bum.

At the library, at that time, Charlie was an employee. As such, he had the responsibility of returning books checked in or misplaced back to their rightful homes on their rightful floors, sections, isles, and shelves. It was monkey's work, and he was paid a monkey's wage. The fact that he performed the task so poorly, and so lackadaisically, led his coworkers and boss to believe that he was in someway mildly retarded. This was the sole reason he stayed around as long as he did.

Charity. Guilt. Equal Opportunity.

Minimum wage for minimum work was all very fair, but it was lacking the flavor Charlie was searching for. That flavor Charlie found in pretending, and through pretending, Charlie discovered Momentum. This is really where it all began.

And the story could have easily begun here, but then we would have missed all the fucking, never mind its quality.

Picking up on the rumor, Charlie made it a reality. With a hop in his step and smiling continuously, he would mumble things like "Nazis killed babies by not loving them physically," and, "The weatherman said it was a top 10 day!" He would tell stories lacking an end or point to no one in particular. He would smile blankly, and wave hello to people he had just spoken to, and generally engage in all sorts of aimless things that those who are mentally retarded rarely in fact do.

While tiring, and offensive, it was entertaining, at least for a while, but soon, as Momentum dictates, Charlie wanted more. Occasionally then, over the noon hour, Charlie would go out front and mingle with the homeless men who'd gather in wait for the 'Sandwich Man'.

This was a portly, middle-aged bible-beater who would come around twice a week in an old ice cream van full of sandwiches and an ear full of the old J.C.

On the side of the van in a sort of 80's shade of pink was painted: JESUS SAVES.

When he drove up, Charlie would transform into a hungry bum and take a sack lunch sandwich and a "God bless you" from the man.

None of the homeless bunch, if they even cared, ever caught on that Charlie was an imposter, so for weeks the game went on.

After the sandwiches, the man would get out of the van and speak to the regulars, which soon included Charlie. They'd get a little Jesus, and then a little God, and maybe a Mary or two before he'd pack up his show and move on.

Following, Charlie would leave the bum he was, go back inside and become what he had been before, retarded.

But several weeks following, Charlie's boss found out he wasn't what he was, or maybe it was that he was in fact what he was, or maybe it was something else, perhaps the simple sight of Charlie having sex with a woman in a library storage room is what brought his boss to fire him on the spot.

The simple answer is usually the least complicated.

And so Charlie's boss discovered him having sex in a storage room with the mother of a child in the summer reading club. The children had just finished being read a bit from Silverstein by a minor local celebrity when Charlie couldn't climax and made the mother late for pick-up. The boss then went searching for the woman who had abandoned her child and found her getting pounded by his retarded book reshelver.

The library has since altered the rules of the summer reading club.

"Jackson," Monroe yells again, and Charlie waits for him to cross the street and catch up.

Although Monroe calls Charlie, Jackson, he knows that's really not his name, although he doesn't know his name is actually Charlie. Either way, Monroe doesn't care. Charlie doesn't know Monroe's real name either.

That's just the way it is.

Names are of little importance in the Brotherhood, as a Brother takes on the name of the street, avenue, or boulevard he's assigned. What you were before the Brotherhood is of very little importance, or interest.

This appeals very much to Charlie.

"Nice night." Monroe said with a smile behind the hood of his jacket.

"Crisp," Charlie said and grabbed Monroe by the hand, shaking it up and down. "Been up to anything?"

"Went to the shelter yesterday."

"The shelter?" Charlie said, surprised. "Spend the night?"

"No, no. I caught a shower, got some food. It's been damn cold lately. Too cold for a skinny bitch like me."

"Indeed. How was it?"

"It was chewy."

"Chewy's nice."

"Chewy is nice."

"Say," Charlie said, "how's Cleveland, do you know? I haven't seen him in weeks."

"He's good actually, still around. I just moved in with him a few days back. And just in time too, the doghouse I shacked in had started leaking from the bottom. I put some plastic down, but then it was just wet plastic I was laying on.

Then I put more blankets down, over the plastic, but then one morning I woke up stuck frozen to the ground. So to hell with that, I said, and then I ran into Cleveland."

"They don't build them like they used to."

"They don't do shit like they used to."

"I suppose not. So how is he? How's Cleveland?"

"He's good, gone a bit sideways though."

"How do you mean?" Charlie asked.

"Crazy. He's strange, different than he used to be, more serious now, sort of jittery too, but it's really not bad, living with him, I mean, its not permanent, you know, sort of makes it easy that way, and fun, knowing its not forever. You'll have to come by later."

"Maybe I will."

"Well, I'll cross my fingers."

Just down the street, a handful of old homeless men were loitering outside a warehouse, *the* warehouse, warming their hands quietly around a fire in a trash bin.

"Brothers," Monroe said, bowing stiffly, sarcastically, as he and Charlie pass by the fire.

"Jackson, Monroe," one of the old ones said smiling, "so whose pecker was up whose ass tonight?"

And you've never seen a bigger bunch of toothless old drunks bent over at the belly laughing and cackling up mucus as Charlie and Monroe witnessed at that precise moment.

The warehouse was nothing more than a shell these days. It had been a Ford factory in its heydays, a coffee plant in its salad years, and a something else after a while of nothing before being gutted several years ago, during better economic times.

The warehouse was to be reconditioned into condominiums for hip, young professionals. But the capital dried up as quickly as it puddled, and three of the five stories were left without windows, just huge gaps framed by brick. The pillars supporting the floors above could be seen from the street below.

Pigeons had carpeted the bottom floor, and hung around to admire their work.

The lot adjacent was a moonscape. The ground had been ripped apart and abandoned by some bulldozers and their friends. Construction barricades still lined the edge while others were lost somewhere in the middle, buried in the snow and sucked down in the mud.

The Brotherhood met on the top floor.

A central stairwell was the only route to the top, as the elevator had been left for dead a decade or two ago.

On these stairs there often crept, crawled and huddled those on the lowest rung, sporting various levels of mental clarity and health after a string of state and federal budget cuts led the psychiatric clinic to close its doors, leaving these poor souls without the medication and counseling they may or may not have needed.

Brothers, both sober and drunk would mix on these stairs with passers-through, homeless men invited to stay a night or two, to rest up for their journeys to Chicago, Sioux Falls, or any other place that they most likely would never arrive.

Out the door in the morning they'll disappear, blown away by the wind to the places they'll never arrive from the place where they'll never be thought of again.

Life is a string of unexplainable luck, or the lack there of.

Inside the warehouse now, there were thirty or so more men talking in little groups. There were folding chairs, like an auditorium, had the chairs been in rows and not strewn about. Down the middle of the warehouse there was a jagged sort of isle with a little makeshift stage formed by a pallet at the end. Just to the side, there was a table with a platter full of chalky white rolls, a coffee cylinder, and a huge pot of soup so thin it resembled tap water, and tasted just the same.

Charlie and Monroe were at this table when a silver-bearded and powerfully built black man walked up to, and stood on the pallet.

This man was Van Buren Boulevard.

If the Brotherhood had a president, or chairman, he would have been it. Rumored to have been a former Black Panther and Nation of Islam hit man, Van Buren, without question, had control over the Brotherhood, since Cleveland's hiatus, that is.

"Everybody, everybody," he said in a deep, booming voice. "Let's everybody shut their shit and come to order."

And everyone did.

Van Buren said a prayer, and the room said, "Amen".

"Now," Van Buren began. "Eisenhower. Eisenhower Ave. You here Eisenhower?"

"Yeah," came a voice out the top of soot filled lungs from the back of the room.

"Eisenhower," Van Buren said, "word is you've been working everyday now for a weeks. Word is you've been aggressive about it too. Following women, pestering men, using language. This true? And no use lying, because I know it is."

"Yeah, its true. Goddamn government cut my disability checks in half again and seems like…"

"You think I give a damn?" Van Buren cut him off. "Boy, I don't give a shit. You don't need more money. Hell, you about the only one here who gets shit for being a half-inch away from retarded, stupid shell-shocked piece of fuck. And you don't need to be making life harder for everybody else. Hell, damn city's all over us already, goddamned beautification bullshit, and you're part of the reason. All of you that go at it too hard, you're not doing any of us a favor being so damned aggressive. Mix it up, shit. Don't stand in the same goddamned place everyday, and don't share your goddamned signs. Hell, most of you are so fucking lazy I doubt you even wipe your asses."

"Easy for you, Van," Eisenhower said. "I've got my rent due, and I got nothing to give 'em. I'm not going back to the goddamn shelter, and I'm not going to sleep on the fucking street, in some fucking dumpster. I'm dying Van. I got cancer. I can't…"

"All right, Eisenhower," Van Buren snapped, "whiny bitch. Tomorrow you and me'll go down and see that sociologist, Dr. Gonzalez at the University. We'll see if he's got any ideas about getting those checks back, all right? And what the fuck you talking about, rent?"

And the room laughed a bit at all of this.

Everyone was aware of Eisenhower's inability to tell the truth and his ability to tell awfully crafted and stupid lies.

Eisenhower sleeps in a car jam packed full of things he's collected and forgotten about.

Suddenly, there was a commotion of voices echoing up the stairwell from the ground floor.

"What the hell is that," Van Buren said as the doors to the penthouse burst open and two of the old men from outside came in, supporting by the shoulders a bloody mess.

"Garfield's dying," one of the old men screeched.

And as he did, Garfield lifted his head to reveal a face made of meatloaf and a nose of string cheese now twisted to the side.

The room gasped.

The people with in the room did likewise.

"What happened," Van Buren hollered over the buzz as he rushed down the isle pushing Brothers out of his way.

"He said something about the police," one of the old men said.

"The police?" someone echoed.

"Took me out of the park in an unmarked…" Garfield groaned, and air escaped with a squeak out the side of his nose. "In the car," Garfield winced and moaned, "took me down to the bridge."

Tears and blood mixed on Garfield's face creating a pink cocktail that steamed down his shirt and ripped jacket, forming a puddle on the floor.

"All right, all right," Van Buren said, taking control, "Adams, you get some rags and vodka, or whatever you've got on your wino ass. You two, get this boy a seat and put a little pressure on his face to stop that bleeding. Garfield, buddy, I'll go with you to the hospital tonight if you think you need to go, and tomorrow I'll go down to the station and find out what the hell went on. Somebody's gonna answer for this shit, don't worry. We'll get an explanation. We'll get it straightened the fuck out."

"Talking isn't going to work anymore," a voice said softly in Charlie's ear.

"Jesus," Charlie jumped, spinning to the side, discovering Cleveland. "Cleveland, Christ! You gave me a goddamned heart attack."

"Hey, Cleveland," Monroe smiled. "I didn't know you were coming tonight."

"Monroe," Cleveland nodded. "How's it been, Jack?"

"Good," Charlie said. "My God, has it been that long since I've seen you? Did you really grow a beard that fast?"

"It has been a while Jack, but once you start getting some hair on your nuts you'll be able to grow a beard too."

And Charlie was lifted off his feet and moved to the side by a force from behind.

"Is that Cleveland," Van Buren's voice boomed.

"I think it is," Cleveland said, looking at himself, examining his arms to be sure and sarcastic.

"Now I wonder what exactly he thinks he's doing here," Van Buren said, holding rage just beneath his skin.

"I'm here for the tour."

"Don't you get smart with me, Cleveland, don't you dare get smart."

"Relax, Van."

"No you relax, Grover. You relax yourself right the fuck out of here, back to the gutter you crawled from."

"Well, hey, the Brotherhood has certainly lost some of its hospitality since I've been away," Cleveland said, still smiling. "Not good for recruiting, Van. I'd think about that."

Van Buren lunged at Cleveland, outweighing him by nearly fifty pounds, and pushed him back several feet. Two, then four Brothers grabbed hold of Van Buren's shoulders and massive right arm just as he reeled back to deliver a blow.

"You the one to blame for this shit," Van Buren yelled, "you to blame for Garfield. Brothers like you, Brothers who think they've got it all figured out, going off, making their own ways. Get the fuck off me," Van Buren strained, flailing his arms and jerking like a bull. "Get the fuck off my back you fuckers."

"Look Van, I didn't come down here to make a big scene, or to get my ass kicked. I just came to pick up a couple of the boys."

"Monroe, Jackson, you two be careful with this snake," Van Buren said. "I don't like you two around him, and I don't want you two bringing him back, you hear?"

"They're free to do what they want, Van, with whoever they want, whenever they want. These boys pay their dues.

They're good Brothers, and you, might I say, have become quite the tyrant in my absence."

"Monroe, Jackson," Van Buren said, "you either escort this rat outside, or I'll do it."

"Oh Van," Cleveland said, walking away, Charlie and Monroe in tow, "it's all changing, you're just too blind to see it. This way is all coming to an end. Your future's got chalk around it, all of ours do."

"You threatening me?"

"No, I'm just clueing you in. You're still a Brother to me, Van. Whether we like it or not, we're Brothers. You'll always be my Brother, and I'll always be yours."

CHAPTER 4

A one-armed bandit is slang for a gaming contraption called a slot machine. These are popular with the grannies by and large.

Charlie once dated a one-armed bandit. This is slang for a girl that has only one arm.

There's a term for when a word has numerous meanings.

"Their, there, they're" are examples of a homonym, but this is something different entirely, and completely beside the point.

The bandit was a friend of a girl that one of Charlie's friends was dating. This was the first year of college, and Charlie was still very much what could be considered himself, although he didn't really know what that was.

This is normal.

Charlie dated the girl three times. Once because he had to, as a favor to his friend, and two times after that because of the size of her mammary glands in relation to the size of the rest of her body.

Charlie wanted very much to see them, and touch them, and maybe put something between them and squeeze them together, but being vomited on in the middle of a dirty kiss during the third date ruled out the possibility of a fourth, no matter what size her boobies were, or how close he was to putting something in between them.

She, this bandit, and Charlie stored her name somewhere he knew he'd forget long ago, was the offspring of a hate filled marriage and the product of a bitter divorce.

Marriage is a contract.

Love is something different. It does not require an attorney at the end.

She lived with her father and drank whiskey like her mother. She hated her parents, and herself, and dropped out of school later that year, and apparently was violently raped and murdered the previous night on her way to a shelter for battered and abused women.

Women, sadly, and sadly common, are assaulted along this road. They are assaulted usually by the men they are trying to avoid, or by men who are in the process of being avoided by other women at the shelter. Sometimes, they are assaulted by men who are simply looking for someone to assault.

Assault means rape for our purposes here.

Rape is a hard word to say.

Monroe was telling a story he heard about the One-Armed Bandit and how they identified her so quickly because of her lack of an arm.

Distinction.

Charlie caught himself thinking then, in Monroe and Cleveland's newest makeshift home, a broken down minivan, that he had never dry-humped anyone before who had been raped and killed. He had also never known anyone before who hated themself more than he hated himself.

Pretending means never having to say you're sorry.

This girl was from a different life that Charlie had all but forgotten, and he didn't know what to think about it all now. All he knew for sure was that he shouldn't be thinking at all.

Momentum.

Cleveland had just come inside the van with a bottle of blackberry brandy.

Momentum.

"This should warm us up," Cleveland said and tossed the bottle to Monroe.

"And these won't hurt for sure," Charlie said and pulled a half pack of cigarettes from his pocket.

Typically, Charlie's not much for the nicotine and booze. He's not much for the low sort of high. The quick winded nausea and slow-brained wit are things ill suited to those who live fast. But on rare occasions, like when pretending to be homeless has you sitting in a freezing cold van with no wheels in a lead-rich field under a billboard in an abandoned industrial zone, certain concessions must be made.

And time slipped by with the three passing the bottle, sharing the smokes, and lounging on bags of stolen sweaters too small to wear.

Monroe had lifted these bags from a Salvation Army drop point without knowing exactly what was inside. The sweaters would have fit 10-year-old girls, and 10-year-old girls they were not.

Monroe was the type to get drunk off nonalcoholic beer, and there's a story about that, but its silly. So in no time he was lit, sweating in the freezing cold and humming the cords he was strumming on a guitar he had found that had no strings.

Through, and on top of all this, Cleveland and Charlie were sitting, facing each other in the spots that should have been occupied by the passenger and driver's seats, speaking in lazy tones and sharing one of the last cigarettes, passing it back and forth like a joint.

"I've never seen a man look like Garfield tonight" Charlie said. "I've never seen a man beaten to deformity."

"We're ugly beneath the skin," Cleveland said.

"We certainly are."

"Its funny how skin makes such a big difference."

"It is." Charlie said.

"Its funny how skin makes some people beautiful and some people ugly."

"It is." Charlie said again.

"We're not beautiful, you and I."

"Not conventionally," Charlie agreed.

"No," Cleveland said nodding, "not conventionally."

"But is it really so important?" Charlie said.

"It seems to be. Jackson, they pay millions to make us feel ugly enough to spend billions to coat ourselves in plastic. In the suburbs they throw brick on the front of houses made of siding to make them look nicer from the avenue beyond the cul-de-sac adjacent the roundabout down the bike path from the strip mall. It doesn't do anything, the brick, it's just a facade, like bleached white teeth in mouths full of cavities, like the spotless kitchen of a failing marriage. Beneath the plastic we're weak," Cleveland continued, "but we're honest, and there's something to be said about that. They'll whitewash us all, Jack, make us into their little white lies."

"Maybe," Charlie agreed.

"Well, maybe we'll have to put a stop to it," Cleveland said.

"Maybe," Charlie agreed.

CHAPTER 5

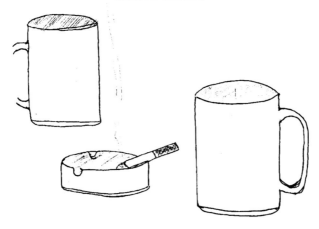

Everyone snaps their fingers. That's what Charlie was thinking on his long walk home from the van, staggering from the chemical mix and fighting off the drunken lazies, lost somewhere between there and here.

In the Puerto Rican projects now, Charlie knew there was a gang of finger snappers in tight jeans not far off. From atop fire escapes with cigarettes dangling from behind greasy mustaches and strutting with flavor down alleys, the Puerto Ricans were patrolling the night.

He knew they were out there, somewhere, waiting for him, but what sort of fantastic dance finale were they planning for his demise? Would he have any chance at all?

It's a dangerous place, drunk, lost, low on Momentum, and not sure what to pretend to be.

Who are you when you're nobody?

Picking up the pace to something close to frantic, and cursing himself for passing out in the van with two bums, he passed an alley and a gated up pawn shop. He passed a newsstand, boarded up and locked for the night. He passed a matted up, skeleton of a dog drinking from an oily puddle in the gutter.

Suddenly, footsteps from behind changed Charlie's lungs to stones, and his veins to something thicker. His hands began to swell. He quickened his pace, but a gear up from frantic is running, and that's risky business when you're drunk, tired, slow and white.

Another ten steps ahead and the feet behind kept falling. Charlie knew it was only one set behind him, so he summoned the courage from somewhere, and turned abruptly to confront the teenage girl behind him.

She was maybe five-two, and probably sixteen.

Her hair was blond, and it was straight, and short. She had it pulled back to the sides, tucked in behind her ears. She looked up, and Charlie caught her sad eyes. They were a blue that was almost gray.

"Hi," she said.

"Why are you following me?" he said.

She was shivering.

"I think I'm freezing," she said.

"I think you are."

"Do you live around here?"

"Not really," Charlie said. "Why?"

"No reason," she said. "There's a diner down the block that never closes. Will you buy a freezing girl some coffee?"

"Okay," Charlie said, having really no idea why.

And so they continued down the block together. She

slid her arm through Charlie's and leaned into him as they walked.

This was a strange and dangerous thing for a strange girl to do, but Charlie felt it was all right, since he wasn't a sexual predator, like everybody else.

"Is this okay? I'm cold."

"Sure," Charlie said, "I'm just glad you're not a bunch of Puerto Ricans."

She nodded against his arm.

The diner they arrived at looked as out of place as the sixteen-year-old girl wrapped around Charlie's arm.

It looked like an old railroad car that rolled off the tracks, tumbled through time and happened to stop right about here, in Chapter 5, sandwiched between apartment buildings.

Inside, there were a few old timers at the counter drinking coffee and reading the paper, or just staring off blankly. They looked like farmers who had followed the railroad car and simply forgot how to get back home.

This happens more than you would think.

There was a line of booths along the wall. Charlie followed the girl to one of them, and sat down across from her.

Before Charlie had really sunk in, a thin and scraggly looking middle-aged man with a cigarette dangling from his mouth, wearing a stained V-neck and an apron around his waist, came over with two cups of coffee. He had some sideburns and a little gray soul-patch holding the skin to his face.

"Thanks, Tom," she said.

"Sure, Liddy."

The man then disappeared around the counter and back into the kitchen.

"You come here a lot," Charlie asked.

"From time to time," she said. "Hot, cheap coffee."

"And your name is Liddy?"

"Lydia."

"That's pretty."

"Its okay. What's yours?"

"Charlie."

"Like Charles?"

"I guess."

"I like Charlie better. It makes you sound a little less like an English princess-killer."

"What?"

"Nothing."

"Lydia," Charlie said, "what are we doing here?"

"Having coffee."

"Besides that?"

"Talking," she said, shrugging her shoulders.

"You know what I mean," Charlie insisted.

"You know, I don't. People talk and have coffee everyday all over the world, Charlie. If you're too much of a freak to take part in this ritual I'll just go to the counter and talk to Tom. It really makes no difference to me."

"Okay, I'm sorry," Charlie said. "It just seems a little strange to be having coffee at what, two in the morning, with a young girl I met following me in the streets in the middle of winter."

"I wasn't following you. I was walking here. I was just walking behind you, and I caught up. Then I invited you to where I was heading, because it's cold outside, and they have hot coffee in here. I'm a bit of an insomniac, and I come in here sometimes when I can't sleep. So are you still paranoid, or are we cool now."

At this point, all the farmers had their necks craned to watch.

"We're cool," Charlie said. "Sorry."

"I think the world would be a better place if it wasn't so uncommon that strangers invited each other to have coffee. There'd be a lot less strangers that way, and a lot more friends."

"I agree with you."

"Good," she said. "Look, I'm going to the restroom now. If you want to leave here's your chance. No hard feelings. Otherwise, drink your coffee and I'll see you when I get back."

"Okay," Charlie said.

Lydia gave a smile and a nod, and slipped out of the booth.

As Charlie sipped and tried to process what had just happened Tom came over to the booth and slid into Lydia's side.

"Cigarette?" he said, as he put another in his mouth.

"Please," Charlie said, although that was about the last thing in the world he needed.

"So," Tom said, flipping Charlie a cigarette and a matchbook, "Lydia give you her 'strangers and coffee' speech?"

"Yeah."

"Fucked up girl, that one."

"Yeah."

"I wish there were more like her. Girls like that," Tom said through a voice box that's tasted too many cigarettes and too much coffee, "they can make a man insane."

"So how do you know her?"

"I think she's my daughter."

"You think?"

"I mean, she might be. I've had a fair number of women for a night or two, and I've got an odd feeling that I've got a kid somewhere in this world that I've never met. She's got a dad somewhere she's never met, or so she says. Universe is a strange place, but it seems to make sense if you look at it from the right angles. She could be my daughter, why not, right?"

"Yeah, I guess."

"Maybe not though," he said, tapping his cigarette on the ashtray. "It doesn't really matter. Its nice to have regulars, whether they're family or not."

"I suppose," Charlie said. "So, you work the graveyard shift here?"

"I work all the shifts."

"But its open 24 hours?"

"That's right."

"So when do you sleep?"

"Who's got time to sleep," Tom said as Lydia returned.

"You harassing my friend, Tom?"

"You bet, Liddy. Hey, nice to meet you. Don't be a stranger," Tom said with a little chuckle and a groan as he slid out of the booth and walked back behind the counter.

"He's interesting," Charlie said.

"Eh," she said, "he's all right."

"So, he's like family to you?"

"I suppose you could say that," she said.

"That's what he said."

"Well he's a little strange, the only person I know who sleeps less than I do."

"So, he sleeps then?"

"I assume so."

And Charlie yawned and took another sip of coffee.

"And I assume you do, too," she said.

"Sometimes," Charlie said.

"Coffee's broken, eh?"

"Apparently," Charlie said and took a drag of his cigarette.

"I wouldn't have pegged you as a smoker." Lydia said.

"I wouldn't have pegged you as an insomniac."

"I don't know, Charlie," she said. "Do you ever feel confined, like there's not enough room to breath?"

"Doesn't everyone?"

"No, I mean, like, what you're doing, and where you're at aren't right for you? Like, life is a pair of shoes, and for some reason you're wearing somebody else's, and they just don't fit."

"Sometimes, I guess."

A more truthful answer might have been: Always.

"I think that when we feel that way, like when we can't breath, it's our biology telling us that this way we're living is wrong. I can't sleep most nights I feel so trapped."

"That sounds like anxiety. There are pills for that."

"There's a pill for every symptom of the disease we've created, but none to cure it?"

"There's no money in a cure." Charlie said. "Treat the symptoms and numb the pain. Its standard procedure."

"Drinking coffee and smoking cigarettes?"

"It's the safest treatment I've found."

"So Tom knows what he's doing after all."

"He just might."

There was a pause then as Lydia sat and stared at Charlie, a smile on her face.

Charlie is a Pretender

Charlie is not a Pedophile.

"I probably should be going home." Charlie said.

"To your wife?"

"No. No wife."

"Girlfriend?"

"No girlfriend either."

"Well, maybe we could go somewhere then."

"Some other time, Lydia. When I'm not sleepwalking."

Charlie laid a few dollars on the table, and slid out of the booth, Lydia in tow. After a nod from Tom the two were back out into the night.

"Do you live far from here?" Lydia said.

"Sort of."

"I'm just a block away. We could go to my place."

"I don't think we should."

"And why not?"

"Because its late." Charlie said.

"What better reason."

"Because your eighteen."

"How do you know I'm eighteen?"

"I don't. I think you're probably younger, but I wanted to be nice."

"I'm plenty old enough, Charlie."

"Maybe."

"Anyway, does it matter?"

"I suppose it shouldn't, but it does."

"Have it your way, Charlie. It'll be your loss. And it's not like I was going to let you do anything anyway."

"Well this way we don't ever have to worry about it. And, it's not my way, Lydia. It's just the way it is."

"Fine then."

"So you're going to be like that?"

"Like what, Charlie?"

"Like you're pouting."

"Anyway," she huffed and shivered, "it was good to meet you. I guess I'm going back inside, by myself."

"It was good to meet you."

"Okay," she said and turned to go back inside, getting a few steps away.

"Hey," Charlie said, "do you have a hat?"

"Like a stocking cap?"

"Yeah."

"No."

"You don't own one?"

"No."

"Do you want one?"

"I guess."

"Well, do you want mine?"

"I can't take your hat, Charlie."

"Well I can't keep it, knowing you don't have one. Besides, I've got plenty. I made my first million in stocking caps."

"In that case, I really am pretty cold. Thank you, Charlie."

And Charlie stepped toward her, taking off his hat.

Handing it to her, she let her fingers hang too long, and sent them sliding slowly along Charlie's palm, and down his fingers.

"Thank you, Charlie." She said softly.

"Don't mention it."

"I won't."

And Charlie smiled sort of sad at this, because it sounded like something he would have said.

"Are you okay, Charlie?"

"No," Charlie said, "I'm not."

He hadn't felt liked in a very long time. He liked this feeling, but at the same time felt ashamed.

Exhaustion, and a mix of chemicals were having a strange effect on him.

"What's wrong?" She said.

"I'm not sure."

It was the awful feeling of a Pretender without Momentum, or identity.

"How do you know anything's wrong then?"

"Because there just is, and you should go back inside."

"I don't want to, Charlie. I want to go with you."

"You should go. I'm tired. I'm not myself."

"You don't really want me to go, do you, Charlie?"

Lydia moved in, putting a hand on Charlie's hip, and raising the other gently to his face.

"No," Charlie said and backed away. "Look, I can't. I'm leaving."

"I think you're all mixed up, Charlie."

"Good night, Lydia."

"Charlie..."

And that was the first time in his life Charlie heard his name said with yearning.

"Good night, Lydia." Charlie said again.

"Good night, Charlie."

CHAPTER 6

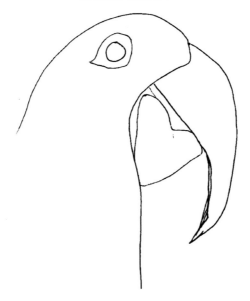

L ock the door, Charlie. Lock the door, Charlie." Sajak said
as Charlie slid past the front door.
Charlie's mother was asleep on the sofa, television
glowing. All the birds were in their draped cages, all but Sajak,
who stood guard, in his cage by the door.

"Lock the door, Charlie. Lock the door, Charlie." Sajak
said twice again, waking Mother out a thoughtless doze.

"Is that you, Charlie? What time is it?"

"It's late, Mother." Charlie said, "I had a few drinks with
my boss."

"That's good, Charlie." Mother yawned loudly. "Being friends with the boss is smart. Make sure you lock the door before you go to bed."

"Yes, Mother. Goodnight."

"Lock the door, Charlie. Lock the door, Charlie."

"Yes, Sajak. Goodnight."

Charlie is planning someday on feeding Sajak to mother in some sort of creamy soup.

It's a quick stop then in his room to strip down to the whities before heading to the bathroom for the evening ritual, and his last bout of the night.

In the bathroom then, Charlie arouses himself to the point of no return. He backs off then at the last second, and drops to the floor for push-ups. He flips over to his back at thirty and does just as many crunches.

Charlie needs to keep the testosterone high. Mrs. Bernstein can't be done on empty.

It's back on his feet then for more rejuvenation, again just to the border, and back down to the floor, with one more set to go.

Try this sometime. You'll hate it.

Charlie does this every night to get through every day.

It's off to bed then, and into a crisp, cold one he slides.

Nighttime is the right time for thinking. On Momentum, thinking is not allowed. Thinking is the avenue to reality. Not where a Pretender wants to be.

Reality is all it seems, but not all its cracked up to be.

Maybe someday, Charlie says quietly, then snaps his eyes closed tight, frustrated by the lapse in composure.

As sleep catches on, exhaustion has him thinking he can almost hear his father speaking with his mother in the front room. They're talking about making dinner. They sound happy. They sound like a family. Charlie drifts away then, feeling skinny and small, thinking of a girl with gray eyes.

It was just the television.

A man was talking about how well his rotisserie oven can cook a chicken, and a woman was having an orgasm while he did it.

Operators were standing by.

CHAPTER 7

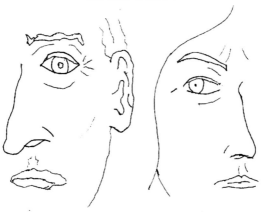

A few days went by, and the calendar got stuck on Monday.

Monday only means something if you want it to. Monday isn't arbitrarily bad. Monday can be great.

Anything is what you make it, or what you pretend it is.

Pretending is similar to lying, in that a lie is true if you believe it. That's how reality works, and so pretending is real if done constantly.

When you stop pretending you start faking, and then you're like most everyone else again.

But it was Monday, and Mr. Bernstein and Charlie were looking at a pistol.

It was Mr. Bernstein's. He purchased it at considerable

expense. It had been the possession of a Nazi who was an officer in the 3rd Reich.

After the First World War there was a Second, and suddenly the First wasn't all that big of a deal anymore.

A roll of the dice placed that officer at an internment camp. It was the same camp that Mr. Bernstein's parents and three uncles were killed by bullets at.

Germans always make decisions during times of war by rolling dice.

Not many people know that.

Nazis kept excellent records. The gun was authentic, as was the bullet still in the chamber.

"Nazis killed babies by not loving them physically," Charlie said.

"I've heard that," Mr. Bernstein said, "and sometimes they just shot them in the head."

"I've heard that, too," Charlie replied, "but there isn't much science involved in that experiment."

"No, but it does take a lot less time."

And Charlie nodded, because that was certainly true.

"This gun," Mr. Bernstein said, and paused long, turning the gun slowly in his hand, "this gun made me what I am."

And Charlie nodded, because that's just what you do.

"You know," Mr. Bernstein went on, "it isn't always the fittest that survive. It's often those who simply find a place to hide."

And a shiver shot up Charlie's spine as a tear rolled down Mr. Bernstein's cheek.

"We all go mad, Charlie," Mr. Bernstein said, "and we all go quite slowly. We don't know it's happening, like we don't feel the Earth spinning, not until we're drunk enough. Charlie, imagine seeing a young child every day for a year, and then going away for five. You knew him well, and now you hardly recognize him. Stay another year then go away again. Then go for ten, then twenty.

"Who is this man in front of you? This man has now lied and he's loved. He's cheated, and been cheated. He's been hurt. He's hurt. He's wanted to die. He's wanted to kill. Maybe he has. Imagine all the things that this little boy now believes as a man. Our boy has gone mad, hasn't he? Charlie, how drunk do we need to be to feel ourselves going crazy? How strong do we have to be to stop spinning?"

That was a lot of words.

And Charlie said, "I don't know."

"I forgot," Mr. Bernstein said, "that's your generation's answer for everything, isn't it?"

And Charlie said, "I don't know."

Which was true. To know he'd have to ask everyone, and not everyone's number is in the phonebook.

Generalizations are generally not accurate.

The front door opened then and Charlie jumped from the table and grabbed the feather duster sitting to his side.

"Hello," Mrs. Bernstein called, annoyed, from the foyer.

"In the study, dear," Mr. Bernstein called back.

"Is Charlie here?"

"Yes dear."

"Then why in the hell is he not helping me with my bags?"

Charlie put down the duster and scrambled into the foyer.

"Sorry ma'am, I was dusting."

"I don't pay you, Charlie, so I can break my back like a goddamn mule."

Mr. Bernstein laughs from his study.

"Yes ma'am," Charlie said, "I apologize."

"Take these bags upstairs to the bedroom, will you, and start cleaning the master bath. The goddamn thing is filthy."

"Yes ma'am, my apologies again," Charlie said and picked up the bags.

"Fine," she huffs, "just do as I ask, Charlie."

Charlie took the bags up to the bedroom, like she said, and started in on the master bath.

He was kneeling, about to begin to scrub the tub when he felt Mrs. Bernstein come up from behind him. He stood up then, bending at the waist, and started scrubbing the tub, just like he knows she wants him to. She came from behind and pressed her body against his. She slid her cold hands up the front of his shirt, going softly over his thin stomach and chest.

She put her arm around his waist and slid her hand down, on the outside of his pants. She found then what Charlie had prepared for her, just as he knew she'd be expecting. She did then what she does for a short while, eventually moving inside and really starting in on the business, until Charlie took his cue, and turned to begin on her.

Soon they were in the bed and he was on his back. She bounced up and down on top of him, her breasts in his face. He pounds, she talks, her dentures lost their grip, and Charlie was back dusting the study in no time.

CHAPTER 8

AGATHA
SENIOR TELLER

S till Monday, still early, Charlie is downtown.
Charlie was on Jackson Street, and was Jackson Street.
He was working.

We all have to work.

But Charlie wasn't paying attention to his work. He was 'phoning it in'. He was searching the masses for a girl with gray eyes. He didn't notice the girl coming his way with brown ones. He didn't see her coming. He asked her for change. He should have known better. She had a child with her.

"I don't have any money," she said, "I'm sorry."

And then this woman did what most people don't, she looked at him, eye to eye, before she passed.

A synapse quick snapped somewhere under her thick brown hair, and after another step or two she craned her neck back to the bum she just passed.

"Do I know you?" She said. "I do, don't I?"

And Charlie was then up to speed.

"I know you from the library," she realized.

"You know me from a broom closet," Charlie said, and forced a smile, clashing with the jitteriness shooting from his eyes.

"Well," she said, and nervously clenched her jaw, pressing her top teeth into her bottom lip, thinking she had had sex in a library with a bum.

"Yeah…" Charlie said slowly, dragging out the word, allowing his head, spinning hard, to come up with some sort of way out.

She let her jaw relax, revealing four little indentations in her lip from the bite.

Charlie licked his bottom lip. He had indentations of his own.

"This is research," Charlie sprang back to life. "I'm at the University. Sociology. I'm working on my thesis."

"Oh," she sighed, and exhaled stronger than respirtoraly necessary, "God, I thought you were homeless."
"Good," Charlie laughed, "then I should have my PhD soon."

And she turned around then, because she was being tugged at.

"Mom?" the little boy nagged in tow, maybe eight years old.

"I'm sorry, Michael."

"This is your son?"

"Yeah. Hey, Michael, I want you to meet a friend of mine," she froze, and smiled sheepishly, sort of like how sheep smile in similar circumstances.

"I'm Charlie," he said.

"Charlie," she repeated, smiling again. "Michael, this is my friend, Charlie."

"Hey," he said, completely uninterested.

"Hi yah, Mike," Charlie said, and waved pathetically to a boy who was looking the other way.

"Michael," she snapped at Charlie, but not angrily. "His name is Michael, not Mike."

"Not Mike?"

"No."

"Not Mikey?"

"No, just Michael."

"Alright, well its good to meet you, Michael."

"Um-kay," he said, still not giving a shit about it.

"And now what's his mother's name?" Charlie asked.

"What?" she said.

"What's your name? I don't know it."

"God, I'm sorry. I'm Agatha."

"Agatha?"

"Agatha Murff," she said and shrugged her shoulders, "that's my name."

"Well, that is a name."

"Excuse me?"

"Nothing, well, it's just, God, that's like the worst name I've ever heard."

"Sweet of you to say. It was my grandmother's name."

"She sounds old."

"She's dead."

"Well that's pretty old." And Charlie cracked the smile his mother gave him.

Agatha smiled back, although she didn't want to.

"So you're a just a part-time bum then?"

"Yeah, I'm trying to go full time, for the benefits, but you know, got to join the Union first."

This was actually not far from the truth.

"Well, it was good and strange to meet you," Agatha said.

"Yeah, I'll look forward to seeing you again at the library."

"How did you know we were going to the library?"

"I didn't. It was a joke. You know, the library."

"Right, very funny. Hey, if you want, you can walk with us."

"Uh, well, you know, I think I actually might. You did blow my cover after all."

"Yeah, that was a joke, too."

"Oh, well, too bad. Let's go."

"Okay, I don't really know you."

"I don't know you either."

"And so us walking together makes sense how?"

"It's complicated." Charlie said. "Lucky for you, I'm a Sociologist. I'll explain..."

Due to time constraints, we're skipping ahead and believing that Charlie gave Agatha an incredibly convincing spiel that would have persuaded even the most distrustful woman that it was okay to walk with her son and a stranger posing to be homeless to the library.

"Okay." Agatha said.

Laziness is the mother of invention.

"Hey, Michael, honey, could you go in front of us a bit? I want to talk to Charlie a little while we go."

Michael rolled his eyes and walked on ahead.

"Thank you, Michael," she called, just like a mother would.

"So," Charlie said, "not Mikey, not Mike, not Mickey, not..."

"Nope, just Michael."

"Huh, professional curiosity, why is that?"

"Well, his father was Mike, Mikey, and all those other names, and all those other things that I hope Michael never becomes. I just want to raise my boy into a Michael, you know."

"I think I get it. And the father, where is the old man?

"Michael's father is no longer my husband."

"I'm sorry."

"Don't be. It was for the best."

"It usually is."

"So they say."

"Hey," Charlie said, "that didn't have anything to do with us, there in the library, did it?"

"No," she laughed, and a little too loudly for Charlie's ego, such as it was, "that had to do with not getting laid in, I don't even know how long, and, if I remember correctly, our little encounter didn't quite quench the thirst, if you know what I mean."

"Yeah. And hey, in my defense, I mean, it was a closet we were in. It wasn't like I had time to let the wine breathe or anything. And, you know, there's only so much I could get done standing in a bucket. I mean, sure, I could have got a little creative with the mop, but I didn't want to scare you."

"Okay, yikes."

"No, seriously, it did have nothing to do with your break-up, right?"

"No, Charlie. You were reading Vonnegut, remember?"

"Was I?"

"Yeah."

"And that was all it took?"

"Sad to say."

Vonnegut usually won't get you laid, but you can try it.

"So when did you and Michael's dad split up?"

"It's been, I don't know, maybe two years now. You know, Michael hasn't even seen his father since then."

"Really?"

"Yeah. He wasn't really around much before that, but two years ago he just sort of left and never looked back."

"Unbelievable."

"Tell me about it."

"Its hard to grow up without a father."

"Michael's okay. He's a good boy."

"I'm sure he is. I'm just saying, I know, it's hard to grow up without a father."

"Your parents divorced?"

"Sort of, my father's dead."

"Oh."

"Yeah, death, divorce, whichever. Sometimes it's the same thing, you know."

"Well, I'm sorry."

"Don't be. I still had a mother."

"How'd he die? Sorry. I'm sorry, that's none of my business."

"No, it's okay. He ate some bad noodles."

"What?"

"Bad noodles." Charlie said. "That's what killed him."

"Noodles?" Agatha laughed. "You're joking, right, please say you're joking. I'm going to feel terrible if you aren't joking."

"Hey, it happens. Noodles can be a killer."

"Oh God," she said, still laughing, "I'm sorry. I've just never heard anything so bizarre."

"Stranger things have happened. Like, I once lost a job for having sex in a closet with a woman whose name I didn't even know."

"Yeah," she said and stopped laughing. "That's pretty bizarre, too."

"It is. Hey, he had a heart attack."

"What?"

"My father, he had a heart attack. The noodles didn't get him."

Agatha then hit Charlie in the shoulder.

"Easy, easy on the Doctor," Charlie laughed.

"You're a jerk, Charlie."

"Then why are you smiling?"

"Because I hate you."

"That's a strange reason to smile, professionally speaking, I mean."

"Stranger things have happened."

"I suppose they have."

"Well," Agatha said, "this is it."

And this was it. They were at the library. Michael had already scrambled up the stairs.

"It was nice to really meet you, Agatha."

"It was nice to really meet you, Charlie. I go by Marie at work, by the way."

"Really? Why Marie?"

"Middle name. I wear a nametag. People usually make clever comments about my dead grandmother when the tag says: Agatha."

"People are jerks."

"Especially to bank tellers. That's what I am."

And there's nothing wrong with that.

"Well," she continued, a quirky little smile on her pretty little face, "I'm a senior bank teller, actually."

"So, that's like management, huh?"

"Yeah, I'm like a V.P. You're a jerk, Charlie."

"Then why are you smiling?"

"Because I hate you."

"Yeah? Hey, I didn't say I didn't like it, your name, well, I sort of did, but, it is original, I'll give you that. I've met a million Marie's, well not quite a million, maybe only seven, but I've only met one Agatha."

"How many Marie's have you met in a broom closet?" She smiled.

"Ha," Charlie laughed, sending a fleck of saliva onto her face that she didn't notice. "Just the one."

And Charlie asked her for her phone number, and wrote it down on an empty pack of cigarettes he picked up.

It was lying atop a heap in a garbage can.

CHAPTER 9

N ext to that garbage can a van pulled up.
On the side, in that 80's shade of pink was written: JESUS SAVES.

Charlie noticed the assembly of homeless coming toward the van from the park across the street.

The park, named President's Park, and referred to by many as Panhandler's Park, was one of the main attractions downtown, or at least it was supposed to be. Surrounded by old brick buildings housing stores and cafes with a backdrop of clean, crisp, towering skyscrapers, it was to be a Mecca for office workers on their lunch hours and families on their weekends. The park offered a healthy mix of treed, flowered and open spaces. A manmade stream populated by hand picked Koi swimming beneath tame ducks and geese wound its way through the park and fed a crescent shaped lake in the middle. The water was then pulled by pumps underground, underneath the lake, and taken back to the beginning, to the perpetual spring.

It was Nature as Man intended.

Again, Charlie was working. He was still in his work clothes.

"Jackson," somebody yelled from the crowd. And that somebody was the nobody named Monroe.

"Hey, buddy," Charlie smiled and grabbed Monroe's outstretched hand, shaking it up and down.

Monroe did not smile back.

"Man, you missed it." Monroe's voice was tense.

"What?"

"You know Filmore?"

"Yeah, Filmore, Fil, sure."

"Well you can forget about him."

"What do you mean?"

"I mean he's dead. He was beaten to death."

"What?"

"Yeah, we all found out night before last. Jefferson found him behind a dumpster. And, the last few days, before Fil, since Fil, other Brothers have been getting fucked up too, just like what happen to Garfield.

"Jesus."

"Yeah, its like we're being targeted. Like we're being hunted down or something."

"No," Charlie said. "Its just frat boys. Just some drunk fuckers. Its Nascar, that's all."

"Don't think so, Jackson. Cleveland doesn't think so either. He split as soon as he found out about Fil. I haven't seen him since. He hasn't come back to the van once."

"You don't know where he is?"

"I know he's looking for the bottom of this. I don't know where, or how, but I know that's what he's doing."

"Hey you guys," the fat man, merry friend of Jesus, yelled from the van. "Are you two hungry?"

"Bologna and cheese, Jackson?" Monroe smiled.

"Yes," Charlie smiled, "that would be splendid, thank you."

"After you, sir."

And then came an hour to forget.

CHAPTER 10

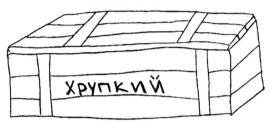

Late on a long Monday, Charlie was close to the warehouse.

He wanted to wipe his ass. He wasn't sure if it was sweat from the quick pace, or if it was a little something else.

Never scratch your hole with your whities.

Mothers tell stories.

A second later, he forgot all about the drips.

Charlie was jolted and pulled by the arm from a hand that flew out of the dark alley he was passing. Spinning toward, and thrown against a wall, the hand jumped up to cover his mouth. The body connected to the hand pressed itself to Charlie, wrapping legs around legs and an arm under the pits and behind Charlie's back, pinning him where he stood.

"Easy Jackson," a voice said softly.

"Cleveland?" Charlie grunted from beneath the hand.

"Hey, buddy," Cleveland whispered. "Sorry for the drama."

He took his hand off Charlie's mouth and backed away.

"What the fuck?" Charlie demanded.

"Quiet." Cleveland said. "That's why I put my goddamn hand on your mouth."

"Why?"

"Come here." Cleveland motioned for Charlie to go to the alley opening. Just down the street they eyed who looked like LBJ, from the Lyndon Baines Johnson expressway off ramp, one of the Brothers specializing in windshield cleaning/handling.

This is generally considered the most annoying form of panhandling. It is also possibly the most dangerous.

Two good reasons why it persists.

LBJ was walking alone.

There was something heavy in the air, and a big old Ford sitting with its lights off a little down the street came to life and went racing toward him, hopping the curb. LBJ fell in terror to the ground, in just the way you would expect a scared old homeless man to. Two thugs with pantyhose over their faces, like bank bandits, jumped out the back and drug LBJ to the car, slamming knees, feet and fists into his face, back and ribs. LBJ was thrown into the back, the doors closed, and the car raced off into the night.

"That would have been you, Jack." Cleveland says, as though he had no emotional attachment at all.

"What the fuck just happened?"

Charlie was mesmerized.

"That's what's been happening, Jack."

"They were just waiting there for him?"

"They were waiting for the first one they saw. We're all the same to them. They get paid no matter who they get."

"They get paid?"

"They're hired, Jack. They're thugs, they're all the same."

"Someone's paying them to hurt us?"

"More or less. Listen Jack, we're not safe just standing here. Follow me."

And Charlie did.

Blind trust is a natural response to shock, as is losing control of one's bladder.

Animals are all the same, no matter what they think of themselves.

Charlie followed Cleveland down the alley, no words necessary. Cleveland was walking with purpose. Down more alleys, and across several streets, trips always seem longest when you don't know where you're going.

Charlie didn't pee his pants earlier.

Down yet another alley, Cleveland finally stopped at a door. Through that door they went, and up several steep concrete stairs. At the top, it was through another door, and they stepped into something completely different.

They were standing at the back of a little restaurant, plastered with Old World charm. Dimly lit, the floors were a dark old wood. The walls were bare brick with plaster clinging here and there. Ductwork hung black, suspended from a once intact tin ceiling.

The restaurant was half full of the middle-aged hip. Little tables were bouncing their little conversations off the walls, mixing with each other, forming an incoherent debate. A few were at a small bar in the middle sipping on their wines and fancy beers, sucking down cigarettes.

A pretty little waitress in her black and whites noticed the two homeless men in the back, and looked on with concern. A thin and balding bartender with little bottle cap eyeglasses then appeared from behind the bar, coming up from somewhere below. As Cleveland and Charlie passed by, he nodded at Cleveland. Cleveland nodded back. Charlie wasn't sure what to make of that.

To the opposite side of the restaurant they were bound, and when they got there they turned a corner and found a wooden staircase, old and warped, and they went down. Beneath their feet the stairs squeaked, sagged and cracked.

At the bottom of the stairs they turned another corner, passing storerooms, a steel-doored freezer, and several cockroaches scurrying to wherever it was they were late for. At the end of the hall, there was another staircase, and again they went down, deep now into the bowels of the city.

At another bottom and down another hall, past a dead rat, Cleveland led Charlie to a room.

It was locked.

Cleveland had the key.

He opened the door and had Charlie go in. The room was dark, and when Cleveland closed the door behind them it was pitch. Seconds later, a cord was pulled somewhere, and then there was light.

"I've caught a glimpse of the future, Jackson." Cleveland said.

"Really?" Charlie said, looking around the room, full of wooden crates with a block writing on them that looked like Russian, backwards and hard angled.

Cleveland sat on one of the crates. Charlie walked toward the middle of the room. The ceiling was leaking behind him.

The room smelled like shit on your hands.

"That's right, and the future I've seen is being planned by those that think they can control it."

"And what's that supposed to mean," Charlie asked. "What's the future?"

"Perfection." Cleveland said.

"And we think there's something wrong with that?"

"Yes."

"What?"

"Us."

"What's wrong with us?"

"Nothing," Cleveland said, "except there is no 'us' in the future. Jack, in their future we don't exist. We've been swept away. Part of their vision of perfection is the elimination of poverty.

"Wouldn't that be a good thing?"

And Cleveland's eyes popped like they were being pulled out.

"No, Jackson," Cleveland snapped, "it would not. Poverty and homelessness are not diseases. Being hungry, being insane, living in the heat, dying in the cold, these are all realities. In their future, there's none of it anymore. There's nothing left. None of us. No reality. Plastic is what they want. And they'll wrap their plastic around us like a snake, and squeeze out every last drop of humanity, until there's nothing left."

"Cleveland, what the fuck are you talking about?"

"Poverty is the foundation of capitalism. Wealth is the penthouse. Poverty is the foundation of humanity. You can't change that, they know it. You can't fix poverty, you can only haul it away."

"And where are they hauling us?" Charlie asked, a bit sarcastically.

"To camps, Jackson. We'll be taken to labor camps."

"Concentration camps?" Charlie laughed. "Oh Cleveland, you're from Montana, aren't you."

There's nothing wrong with Montana.

"Jackson, I've seen the camps. They already exist."

"What do you mean, you've seen them?"

"Well, one of them. In Kansas."

"Kansas? What the fuck are you talking about?"

"I'm talking about Garfield."

"Garfield?"

"Yeah, Garfield, and Filmore. I'm talking about LBJ. I'm talking about you and me and Monroe, and Van Buren and Johnson, Washington, Adams, Roosevelt, and everyone else who is with us at the bottom."

"What did Van Buren ever find out from the police about Garfield?"

"What do you think? They took a report. Charlie, the police have nothing to do with any of this. Not yet anyway, not officially. They won't be involved until much later. Van knows all this. He's seen the camps too. We saw them together, but he's too frightened to believe its true, or to do anything about it."

"Cleveland, seriously, this idea you've conjured..."

"First," Cleveland cuts off, "we'll be hounded in the streets. There will be attack, after attack, after attack. Then, we'll fight back. Or so it would seem. It'll be staged. Something big will happen, and they'll pin it on us. Then the police will enter, and clear the city of the homeless menace, making it safe for all the good, hard working taxpayers to live happy, productive lives.

"Then, we'll be in the camps, 'bettering ourselves', getting 'job training'. It'll be billed as a welfare reform, and it will be spectacular. We'll be taken away, and no one will ever see us again, because we will cease to exist. Their pinstripes will become our prison bars. Poverty will eventually become an idea, and that idea will eventually be forgotten, and it'll take compassion right along with it. Life will succumb to little more than an arms race for possessions."

"What do you mean something big will be staged?" Charlie said.

"Well, I don't know how big it will be. I mean, it could just be something like a burned down pawnshop or bar, something like that, something no one will miss, something that they'll tear down eventually anyway. They'll kill two birds with one stone. Then they'll have us assaulting people in the streets, and we'll be turned into an epidemic. Are you following me?"

"Oh, I'm following you. Cleveland, this is all terribly far fetched."

"I know it is," Cleveland said. "You're exactly right. That's one of the main reasons it might just work. That, and no ones really going to care what happens to us, as long as we're gone."

"So what are you proposing to do?"

"Not wait for them to set us up. If our future, if our distinction is inevitable, we might as well make it interesting. I say we take the blindfold off this city. If we hold this place up to a mirror these people will not like what they see. They don't know what they've become. They can't see how mad they've turned. We need to show them. Everything they're trying to do, the clean up, the building, the beautification, everything they're doing, it's all a cover-up. It's a mask for their ugliness. It's a tint to cover the pimple. It's the girl with big tits and a bag on her head. It's plastic, Jack, and we're going to rip it off and show them what's beneath."

"So you're a terrorist now?"

"There's nothing more terrifying than the truth to people content with a lie. Enlightenment and terror are the same thing, it just depends on who you're talking to, and which side you're on."

"Cleveland, you've gone crazy."

"Maybe, but how crazy are you? How crazy can you stand to get? How much of yourself are you willing to lose to get to the greatness underneath, beneath all the plastic? The Brotherhood is crumbling, Jack, but I'm collecting all the pieces, and am building us an army."

"An army of homeless men."

"That's right."

"The girl with big tits and a bag over her head?"

"Yeah," Cleveland chuckled, "I was running out of things to say."

"It had to happen eventually."

"So are you in or what?"

"Of course I am."

Momentum.

CHAPTER 11

Rules make cheating possible. Rules make someone right, and someone wrong. Rules make some of them winners, and most of us losers.

Relationships between women and men are sadly similar. Pure and open honesty leaves no mystery, and is not well suited for the strain of curious apes that wants what they don't have, whatever it might be.

It was a Friday, and Charlie had yet to call Agatha Murff. That's five days. This is long by most standards, but Charlie had been preoccupied with revolution, and going to college and working nights, and being a housekeeper, being a prostitute, an adulterer, a son, a bum, and a young man, lost and alone.

Fiction can take up a lot of time.

Every night he looked at the number on the pack of cigarettes. Every night he looked at the numbers on the phone. His fingers knew the movements, he'd been dialing the digits in his head since he got them. He'd lay in bed, trying desperately not to think, but couldn't stop himself from wondering. He wanted to speak to her, to get to know her, to see her, to be with her, to maybe know her son, to maybe...

And this was as far as he ever let it go. What he wanted was impossible. Pretending would never allow something so real. Momentum would fade, and never return. And then what?

What is it that the real people do?

Nevertheless, this was becoming Charlie's silly little dream.

There's nothing wrong with that.

But on Friday he called her. She pretended she wasn't pissed off for being made to wait so long. She pretended she didn't care if he called or not, like she hadn't even thought about it.

Women.

Charlie lied something about throwing away the pack of cigarettes, forgetting the number was on them, and then having to drudge through the coffee grounds, paper towels, and apple cores to get it out. This made Agatha laugh. Charlie thought it might.

Men.

Most relationships start off with alcohol, and this one would be no different.

Charlie drove his mother's car, which hadn't been driven in months. It was a solid tank of a Buick, which perhaps was the reason it hadn't been driven in months.

Charlie let the thing warm up about ten minutes as he decided what tape, and what song to have on when he picked up Ms. Murff.

And here goes nothing.

Charlie put the bucket in drive, and it rolled slowly out the garage, moving like a sore old man lathered in BENGAY and Vicks Vapor Rub.

Agatha was about 20 minutes away, and not the good way. Agatha and Michael didn't have a lot of money, and they didn't flaunt the little they had. They lived close to public housing.

The apartment building that was their home was directly across the street from a little hole in the wall, crack in the window biker bar, The 69er.

It was on 69th Street.

College boys, and other silly little men will hear of this bar and go from time to time, possibly searching for something stupid to boast about to their friends back home in wherever, or maybe just looking to purchase a clever t-shirt, but they generally never stay long, if they even go in at all.

To the disappointment of the brave souls that do enter, there are no t-shirts for sale.

There was a spot right in front of the building. Across the street chopped up hogs lined the curb.

Agatha was waiting inside the security door.

She saw Charlie pull up in a mule, and give himself what looked like a pep talk before he got out. Charlie didn't know he was being watched, and Agatha didn't know whether this was cute or weird, or whether he was just listening to music. She decided it was a pep talk. She assumed it was cute, but reserved the right to change her mind at any time.

Michael was also watching, four floors up. He couldn't see the pep talk, which was good, because it was definitely more weird than cute.

Agatha's neighbor was watching as well. She couldn't see much of anything at all, but she's old, and that's normal.

Charlie got out of the car, and saw Agatha coming toward him. She was wearing a sort of orange, fuzzy sweater and jeans under a charcoal pea coat. It was a very simple little number, but it did the trick. Her thick brown hair was down, and lying politely behind her shoulders. Charlie couldn't tell if she was wearing any makeup.

For some women, that's supposedly the goal, to make it look like you aren't wearing any. For others, apparently, it's to wear as much as physically possible.

Charlie had on gray running shoes, dark green/gray sort of pants and a black cotton sweater over a red striped collared shirt.

The collars stuck out of the sweater and rested on his collarbones.

Collared shirt. Collarbones. Collared greens.

English is fun.

Originally, he thought the shoes made him look clever. Now he wasn't so sure that was the look for him.

"You look nice," Agatha said as Charlie got out of the car to meet her, and fetch the car door.

"*You* look nice. *I* wore running shoes."

"Who cares? I'm the one who looks like a pumpkin."

"Most people like pumpkins, I mean, pumpkin pie, who doesn't like that? And pumpkin...uh," Charlie was at a loss, "I guess that's about it, huh, pumpkin pie? Well, people like pumpkins anyway, for decorating and other things probably. Maybe we should go now, before I keep talking."

"I think that'd be wise," Agatha said through a smile, "for you anyway. I may be screwed either way here."

"Well," Charlie said, and for some unexplainable reason decided to turn Scottish, "we didn't a' get dressed up for nothing."

He wasn't pretending to be a dork. He really was one.

And Charlie walked her to the car and opened her door.

"So, Braveheart?" She said, sitting down into the car.

"Yeah, I don't know what just happened," Charlie said and shook his head in shame. "Sometimes I just blackout."

And a snort came from somewhere inside Agatha's little body.

"I think you just sat on a pig," Charlie said and closed the door promptly, and set off around the back of the car.

It looked like she was smiling.

It's surprising the things you think you can see by looking at the back of someone's head.

"Its my mom's car," Charlie defended as he slid in.

"Hey, a car's a car," Agatha said.

"Yeah, but I think that reasoning only works when you're in high school."

"Maybe."

"So, I thought we'd get a little drunk before dinner. I'm not going to take you anywhere fancy, so a little buzz might make you think you're somewhere nice, which would be good for me."

"Oh, you think so?"

And Charlie simply nodded. He was doing good so far, or at least he wasn't doing terrible. He had done a lot worse.

One time he went out with a girl with one arm and big jobbers that vomited on him when his tongue was in her mouth.

That was pretty bad.

Rest in Peace.

That was worse.

The car rolled off, now eligible for the carpool lane, had there been one.

The music was perfectly cued and went unnoticed.

And they made their way into the hip little downtown part of the city where the people with lawnmowers don't live.

On this way Charlie and Agatha noticed how little they knew each other, only having had sex once and a couple brief conversations. They found themselves talking about work.

This is just about as bad as being vomited on.

Agatha agreed with that, and didn't say too much about it. It was just a job, a paycheck, and nothing more. She was more interested in the young Doctor of Sociology.

"The homeless," Charlie said, "are the foundation of capitalism. They play a vital role in the physical and psychological structure of society. Would wealth really exist without poverty?" he asked.

Agatha's bottom lip disappeared and she gently shook her head.

Charlie was pleased at her boredom. It meant he was playing his part well, because really, would anyone normal honestly care?

He steered the conversation then to topics surrounding Michael, Agatha's son.

Charlie can't remember much about being a boy, and its something he's grown out of being able to pretend.

The fact that Agatha was raising a boy on her own greatly impressed Charlie, as he found the idea of parenting absolutely horrifying.

He was open to the idea of mating however.

Besides, it's a safe bet that a mother will always want to talk about her children, typically to the point where you never want to hear about her stupid little kids ever again.

Agatha didn't succumb to this. She kept the summary of Michael's life short and light.

Soon Charlie was searching for a spot big enough to hitch the beast, and in no time they were making their way down cobblestone streets past dozens of little restaurants, bars and shops. They stopped in a plush bit of a bar full of young professionals still dressed for work on a Saturday night.

The bar resembled a lawyer's study, accented with bookcases, wood grain and leather. There was a baby grand piano in the back, collecting dust.

The two sunk into a little setup in the corner, away from the young brokers, bankers and various levels of office staffers.

There's nothing wrong with these people, until they skull fuck your grandmother with jargon she'll never understand to sell her peace of mind.

But it's just business. It's nothing personal.

Generalizing makes everyone equal.

Charlie ordered a bottle of red wine with an artsy type of rodent looking something like a raccoon on the label. It came recommended by the girl that charged them for ordering it. And as they bled that bottle dry they spoke about the things they wanted to and blinked to keep their eyes from turning into cotton balls.

A good bottle of wine can have that effect on two people.

A cheap bottle of anything can have that effect as well.

So after the tip and on their way, they walked beneath the streetlights and the clear black sky toward the night's restaurant just a few blocks down. Their shoulders rubbed occasionally as they walked down wide sidewalks.

"Look at those two," Charlie said, pointing to their shadows stretching in front of them. "They look happy."

And the bigger shadow took the other by the hand, and they did then look happy.

They looked like a giant 'M'.

And everything changed a second later, as everything always does as long as you keep moving. The light they were approaching became stronger than the light they were leaving and the happy shadows jumped behind them and were all but forgotten by the two drunk kids who left those bastards in the dust.

Momentum.

"Have you ever been to La Châteaux," Agatha asked, and Charlie forgot what it was that he was about to say, and said instead, "No," and he thought he was telling the truth. "I've heard about it though," he said, "is it down around here?"

"Yeah, its right here," she said and stopped abruptly. And it was in fact right here, and they were in fact right there. She wasn't lying. "I've never been either, but I always wanted to."

"Always?" Charlie said.

"Always," Agatha nodded.

And Charlie had heard of it. He heard it was a fancy little hole full of pretentious twenty-something's and older, equally pretentious, but honest to God wine connoisseurs who could actually afford the medium and therefore earned their right to be pretentious.

But this was all hearsay, and stereotyping. The patrons could simply be a bunch of nice Baptists who just like wine. Or, maybe they weren't religious at all. You never know with Baptists.

"It wasn't where we were thinking about going," Agatha said, putting an emphasis on the word 'going', turning the sentence magically into a request that she knew full well would be granted, "but..."

"Only because I didn't know where it was," Charlie interrupted. "I'm sure they've got bread or cheese or something."

"I'm not really hungry," she said. "I just want some more wine."

And Charlie wasn't about to argue with that.

So they did walk into that fancy little hole to sit among those that probably were not Baptists.

Not hopping, but busy, maybe three people were working. The place was dimly lit. The floors were a dark old wood, and the walls were bare brick with plaster clinging here and there. Ductwork hung black, suspended from a once intact tin ceiling.

Conversations bounced off the walls and ceiling, mixing with each other, forming an incoherent debate. A few were at a small bar in the middle sipping on their wines and fancy beers, sucking down cigarettes. Little tables surrounded the bar that were capable of sitting three to five comfortably, and about half of the tables were busy doing just that.

Our heroes choose a table that was empty.

Anything else would have been a little awkward.

"I'm not sure exactly what we want." Charlie said when the twenty-something, bushy-haired, scenester styled waiter walked over and poured two glasses of ice water.

"What did we have at the first place," Agatha said.

"I think it was a cabernet," Charlie said, "a cab, I don't really remember. You want to stick with that?"

The waiter swayed back and forth impatiently. He wanted to finish the cigarette he just started at the bar.

"Yeah," she said, "I think it was a cab. There was a rat on the label."

"I thought it was a possum. Well," Charlie smiled, "it looks like we want a cab with a rodent on it."

"Yeah, gonna have to be a little more specific there," the waiter said, not in any sort of jovial mood, "we have about a hundred."

That's a lot of rodents.

"Well," Charlie said, smiling off the rudeness, "are there one or two in particular that you'd recommend?"

And the waiter exhaled though his nose and shook his head, not at all trying to hide his contempt for people who didn't know everything.

"Look," Agatha interrupted, "the more we spend the less we'll tip. Just don't give us the swill."

"Okay," the waiter said, and for a second became a real person, "there's a Cotes du Rhone I can bring you. Its like thirteen bucks, plus the cork fee. Can't really go wrong with that."

"Sounds good," Agatha said both quiet and sweet, "thank you," and the waiter smiled a touch and walked away.

"Not bad," Charlie said, realizing he was sitting across from a pretty cool girl.

"What can I say," she replied, "I'm a bank teller."

Just a minute later the waiter returned and without a word uncorked the bottle and poured two glasses, leaving the bottle between them, skipping the whole taste it and tell me if you approve dance.

"Thanks for taking me out," Agatha said.

"Thanks for coming with," Charlie said, and clanked his glass against Agatha's like a big moron.

Agatha smiled, just like Charlie thought she might.

And happiness prevailed for a second or two, until Charlie felt a soft breath in his ear and heard a voice creep gently into it.

"Tell him everything is ready," is what that voice said in something softer than a whisper.

Charlie turned then, and saw a thin, balding man with bottle cap eyeglasses, and suddenly he realized where he was. Charlie had been here once before. He had been in the basement.

The man patted Charlie on the back then and headed for the bar. Behind the bar, in the way back, Charlie saw the door he had entered with Cleveland that night not so long ago.

He turned a few degrees and saw the steps leading to the basement and sub-basement.

Rats, roaches and a stomach now full of cramps.

Charlie did not feel well.

"Do you know him," Agatha asked, not making out what the bartender had whispered.

"No," Charlie said, thinking quick, "he just apologized for the waiter."

"Well, that was nice," she said.

When there's a woman involved, Fight or Flight gets a little more complicated.

"Agatha," Charlie said, "I've got to check my messages."

"Okay."

"My mom's been sick."

"Oh, I'm sorry."

"It's okay. I'll be right back."

Charlie bumped the table as he got up, spilling a little wine and turning a few curious heads.

"Sorry," he said, and walked briskly out the front.

Charlie felt drunk. He felt the world spinning. He felt his stomach whirling, blending everything inside.

He couldn't breathe.

Once outside he realized that maybe he shouldn't be outside, that he shouldn't be anywhere at all.

The terrors of paranoia had hit.

He darted into the alley just a few doors down. He crouched against a wall, out of view of the street.

This had never happened. Lives had never crossed like this before. He'd never been in anything this close to a pickle. He did not like it, not even just a little bit.

Mother is sick, he decided. He had to go to her. He had to go right now.

He got back inside the bar. Agatha's glass was approaching the bottom.

"How's your mom?" Agatha said as Charlie sat down.

"She's not good."

"What's wrong?"

"They're not sure. Its like the flu, but it isn't getting any better. And now she's having side effects to the meds, so that's complicated things that much more."

"Do you need to leave?"

"I'm sorry. We probably shouldn't have gone out tonight. I just wanted to see you again."

"Charlie, you've got to do what you've got to do. She's your mom."

"I'll make it up to you."

"Its okay."

"No, I'll make it up to you."

"Charlie, it's really not a big deal. It's getting late, anyway. I should probably be getting back to Michael."

Charlie felt like the biggest piece of shit on the planet.

One hundred and fifty pounds is a tremendous amount of shit.

Charlie stood up then and laid a $20 on the table.

"Shall we?" He said.

On their way out the door Agatha commented on the Cotes du Rhone. She thought it was real decent.

Charlie hadn't even had a sip.

CHAPTER 12

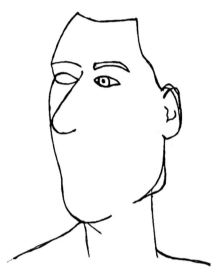

A quiet drive is a strange one, and perhaps a little creepy when the girl doesn't really know the guy who's driving in silence.

Silence is unsettling for the talking strain of apes.

Charlie was busy with self-talk, calling himself a dumb ass and saying the word 'fuck', repeatedly.

"Hey," he said, deciding to interrupt the silence of his internal monologue with a lie, "I'm sorry, I'm just preoccupied with my mom."

"Charlie, its okay. Look, I had fun tonight. Got a little

drunk, had some conversation not with a coworker or an eight-year-old. It was all right. Besides, now we can skip the whole awkwardness of you thinking you're going to get invited upstairs to have sex."

"What?" Charlie said. "You mean we're not going to have sex?"

"No Charlie."

"Well you owe me twenty bucks then."

"God," Agatha laughed.

He looked over at her, and with the streetlights brushing past her face, pointed straight ahead, she looked like something out of an old movie. She had a sort of skewed sophistication and strength that most women Charlie has ever known simply don't possess. She was a kind of simple that you might never understand.

Charlie didn't want to lie to her anymore, so they rode on in silence.

Arriving at the apartment, Charlie couldn't decide if he should leave the car on or turn it off. Safest to leave it on, he decided. If his mother's phony illness was a large enough issue to end the date, it should be large enough to do a simple drop and dash.

He left the car on, but threw it in park.

"Again," Charlie said, "I'm sorry to have to end the night like this. I was having fun."

"Again," Agatha said, "Its okay. I was having fun, too."

And it was strange and silent for four beats until Agatha said, "Well," which took strange up a notch to weird.

"So," Charlie volleyed back.

"Okay," she said, game, set and match, and reached for the handle, leaning toward the door. Charlie reached for her, and brushed her arm gently with his fingers to get her attention.

It did.

He leaned toward her. She leaned back into him, hesitating twice. Charlie's hand moved gently to the side of her face, fingers curling softly round the nape of her neck. She moved her hand to his arm cautiously.

They kissed.

It was simple.

Lips touched, held, and touched again.

A space appeared, then disappeared, as they came together. Mouths opened slightly, and tongues touched shyly, like the first wave of the tide rolling in. The moon pulled, and tongue rolled over tongue. Switching sides on a second to breathe, noses excused themselves.

Levers inside flipped on and dials began to spin. Sparks flew and snapped as two lives got a little more complicated.

Shallow breaths now, blood feasting on a limited supply of oxygen.

Agatha pulled away.

"I should get upstairs, Charlie." Agatha said with her eyes closed.

"Yeah." Charlie conceded.

"Thank you for taking me out, Charlie."

"Thank you for letting me."

"Call me." She said.

"Tomorrow," fell from Charlie's mouth.

CHAPTER 13

On the ride home, Charlie's mind wandered every which way, as did his route.

Charlie found himself lost.

That's a strange place to be.

Creeping slow in a Buick down broken streets he didn't know, Charlie knew for certain that anything could happen.

He saw a van then, a converted ice cream truck, with the words JESUS SAVES on the side written is a sort of 80's shade of pink.

It was under a streetlight.

As he drifted by, he noticed a sign on the windshield. He read it in his rearview mirror. The letters appeared backwards, but it was a simple line.

FOR SALE

God was going out of business.

A thousand thoughts jumped instantly at Charlie's head, but only one grabbed hold.

Charlie is a Pretender.

Charlie is on Momentum.

Tomorrow he will pretend to be something new.

This should be fun.

CHAPTER 14

Waffles popped out of the toaster and Charlie buttered them up, just how Mother likes them. No syrup, just some butter.

The simple pleasures are the easiest to satisfy.

"Thank you so much, Charlie." Mother said.

"You're welcome," Charlie said. "Mother, I've got a busy day ahead of me. I should get going."

"You're not going to eat breakfast with me? We always eat breakfast together."

"I know, Mother. I'm sorry. I've just got a lot I need to get done today, that's all. I'll be home for dinner."

"Okay, Charlie," Mother said, and with slouched shoulders she ate her waffles in silence.

Losing the simple pleasures can break your heart.

Charlie didn't notice Mother's defeat, or say goodbye for that matter, as he grabbed his copy of the Bible on his way out the door.

The Bible was his grade school's gift to him on the day of his eighth-grade graduation. The name of the school was printed on the front. It was meant to be a very special thing.

Charlie put the Bible in his bag and headed off to the Bernstein's for some dusting and fucking.

When he completed his sins, sinking deeper into another fault line, he tunneled on to the next.

He wasn't quite sure where he left it last night, the idea he had that would wind up changing everything. It was parked somewhere between here and there. And he took the bus as far as one should. It didn't go where he wanted, but were he was heading busses don't routinely stop.

Charlie was well off into the wastelands now, the area that exists between a downtown and the start of something else.

He was traveling incognito, with stocking hat, sunglasses and a high-collared overcoat, borrowed from his dead father. He needed to hide himself from any Brother he might come across.

The Brotherhood works downtown, but they don't have to stay there. Some hit it in the morning and afternoon rush, some just in the afternoon, some just in the morning, some will sit there all the goddamn day, and others will simply roam, scavenging cans, seeing old friends, taking in the day and laying in the park, but probably not today.

Today there's a cold wind jumping out from downtown. By the time it gets down to Charlie it's a swirling mess, playing with his pant legs and shoving him around, turning him at times into a kind of mime, walking in place.

He had to retrace the steps of his tires from last night, which is hard to do at a slower speed and the perspective of feet opposed to seat. He was too strange last night from the rattling crazies and whirls of emotion to remember it clearly, so he went back toward Agatha's apartment, where it all began.

He also needed to hide from Agatha, although he didn't want to, but now was not the time for thinking.

Momentum.

After quite some time the apartment building was in sight, a speck in the distance, and he'd decided he'd gone far enough. He swung a corner and went down half a block. Things suddenly looked familiar, but not altogether right. And then, just as suddenly, everything felt wrong.

He was lost, and everyone knew it.

People who usually mind their own business were eyeing him, peering down through old, warped windows and behind twisted, rusted out fire escapes. Their eyes peeped out from behind torn shades and between broken mini-blinds.

They looked like cheap Picasso prints.

The neighborhood was a mix of light and dark-skinned African Americans.

In America we don't judge on the basis of pigment. If you're not white, you're just not white.

We keep it simple so as not to question it.

The silent alarm had been triggered. There was a stranger in the kingdom.

And now, as everyone saw, there were two men trailing that stranger. Charlie felt it, and picked up the pace. He was on the wrong block. That was certain. He sped along, turning this corner and that. He heard himself being called, assuming, "Hey, hey you," meant him.

Charlie tried to pretend that they weren't shouting at him, but fear is a hard thing to work through.

"White boy," the other one said. "I know you can hear us."

Charlie proved them right by stopping, and turning to face them.

"You got some change for a twenty," the first one said.

He had dark skin, was medium built, and by the scars on his face he appeared either to be the veteran of a knife fight or an abusive parent. Possibly both.

We'll call him Scarface.

The other dark-skinned gentleman was well on the heavy side, and this changed the way words sounded coming out of his mouth, making everything a bit garbled.

We'll call him Chubs.

The white skinned gentleman, Charlie, well, we should all have a pretty good idea about him by now.

We'll call him Jesus.

No, we better not do that.

"You got some change," Chubs said.

"No," Charlie said, patting his front and back pants pockets, "I'm broke."

"Shit," Scarface said, "white boys don't come down here with no cash."

"Well I did." Charlie said.

"Then your honky ass is on the wrong side of the tracks, cuz," Scarface said.

"Apparently," Charlie responded.

Here comes some slang, and a bunch of the F-word

"What? You got beef," Chubs said and pushed Charlie in the chest, sending him back-peddling a few steps.

"No." Charlie said. "I don't have any beef. I'm fine."

"Cause we can handle this," Chubs said. "We can squash the beef."

"I'm sorry," Charlie said. "I don't want any trouble."

"Well you in the wrong neighborhood then," Scarface said.

"Yes," Charlie said, "you've made that abundantly clear."

This was probably not the right time for sarcasm.

"Look," Charlie said, "I'll just be on my way."

That was when Scarface recoiled and tagged Charlie square in the jaw. Charlie fell back dazed, then turned to run, but Chubs took him down like government cheese.

That must mean he tackled him.

Scarface gave Charlie a couple kicks to the ribs as Chubs went searching for a wallet that wasn't there.

"This fucker wasn't lying," Chubs said. "He don't got shit."

"Check his fucking bag."

"You check his fucking bag. I'm holding the fucker down."

"Shit," Scarface said as he unzipped it, and pulled out the contents. "All this little bitch got is some dirty clothes and a fucking Bible. Shit, the fucker's a goddamned Mormon."

"I tried to tell you," Charlie said, beneath nearly 300 pounds of thyroid dysfunction.

"Ain't no body talking to your Mormon ass," Scarface said as he stood up and landed a kick to Charlie's arms, now covering his ribs.

Chubs pushed on Charlie to get back to his feet, before donating a kick of his own.

"Fucking no money, no watch, no nothing," Chubs said as he and Scarface walked away.

"Don't let us see you back here again, broke-ass mother fucker," Scarface called back.

Charlie gave a little wave, assuring them that the message was clearly conveyed.

Charlie pulled himself from the ground, repacked his bag and continued to walk, trying to sort through the thoughts and emotions as quickly as possible to get back to live footage.

Words like, nigger, popped into his head. Feelings like hate slipped into his conscious. No, Charlie told himself. Don't think about it, just feel it, and move on. Let it happen, then let it slip away.

Momentum.

The mind is too precious a piece of real estate to be packed to the brim with garage sale memories of unimportant things that you can't shake, or stand to part with.

Momentum.

Charlie kept his wallet at home, and his money in his underwear. A quick check convinced him that everything was accounted for; he was just going to be a little sore in the morning.

Charlie smiled to himself, turned another corner, and saw it dead ahead.

Looking pathetic in late winter, it was a van, an ice cream truck, and it was for sale. Beneath the sale sign in the window there was a small scrap that he didn't see last night. It read, BUZZ JOHNSON, and had an arrow pointing to the left, to a building that boasted rooms rented weekly and monthly in a red neon that threatened to burn a hole through your retinas if you didn't turn away in time.

Charlie walked up to and around the van, checking for rust, and kicking the tires, because that's just what you do.

Completing his lap of automotive inquiry, he walked into the doorway and saw in front of him a panel of buzzers. There were 10, but only one had a name, and that name was Johnson.

He gave it a push, and in a second came a nervous reply. "Go away, please," a man said, and that was it.

Charlie sat there a second. His face turned strange, and his eyes rolled from side to side as though he was on television, overacting confusion. He pushed the button again and spoke.

"Sir," he squeaked, "I'm here about the van."

And a minute of nothing passed, and he buzzed Johnson again. After a minute more, he was rattled. This was unexpected, and not in the good way.

He walked back into the street. Momentum dripped as sweat out of his pores.

Pimples formed and would present themselves in the morning.

His ribs began to ache and his jaw began to throb.

Charlie took a seat on the curb by the van, realizing instantly that he had sat in a bit of water he hadn't seen. With a wet ass he stood back up and sat on the van's back bumper, which broke free immediately, falling with a hollow and rusty clump to the concrete street.

Charlie exhaled, feeling a little sad, a little defeated, and very stupid. He didn't know what to do next. He was beginning to think that he had done the wrong thing in coming.

Which of course he did, but he wasn't thinking in that particular, my school is printed on the Bible in my backpack-I just committed adultery with a sixty year old-and my entire life is a lie sense. It was nothing like that.

But he began to turn on himself.

He took a look around. Nothing made sense.

There was a pain in his chest.

Life felt like it had hit an end. For the first time, since the ride began, life felt like something.

It felt awful.

He stood up, and was just about to leave, just about to wake up, just about to go home, just about to go back to school, just about to get a career, to go to church, to really take care of his mother, to let himself be loved by anyone that wanted to, to begin the life he knew he was supposed to live, but that was when the door opened. That was when a paranoid, fat man in a bathrobe looking out the crack in the door with a baseball bat hidden poorly behind his back said, "You're here for the van?"

That was when Charlie answered, "Yes, I am."

CHAPTER 15

"Well," Charlie said, sitting in an orange chair purchased from a thrift store by the previous occupant and left behind at the time of his eviction, "it was Jesus Himself who brought me to the Cross." The fat man was nodding in utter delight, the springs in his old plaid hide-a-bed wincing with each bounce. "It was Jesus who revealed Himself to me. It was Jesus who gave my life meaning. It was He who led me out of the dark."

"Peter," he said, and that's what Charlie had the man calling him, "thank heaven you came along. I had begun to lose hope. I had begun to think the world had turned it's back on Salvation, turned it's back on Christ."

"It's always darkest before the dawn, Paul." And that's what he had Charlie calling him. In Charlie's days at the library he had never learned the fat man's name, and he, it seemed, had never learned Charlie's face. "Things aren't as bleak as that, I'm certain. Don't lose faith."

"I know Peter, I know. It just doesn't seem fair. I've sacrificed so much to spread the Word. I quit a decent job. I donated away all my trappings and possessions. I rid myself of everything that interfered with my Ministries, and still it wasn't enough. Now I have nothing but debt, and shame."

"Christ knows what you've done, Paul. And you still have all you need."

"I know Peter, I'm just upset. I'm afraid I was just too weak to carry the banner for Christ."

"The banner is heavy," Charlie said, "maybe you bore it long enough. You've given a lot. Today, you're giving me something that I can continue. Your Ministry won't die. You see yourself failing, I see you inspiring."

"Thank God for you, Peter."

"Thank God for you, Paul. Now, should I make the check out to Paul Johnson?"

"My name isn't Johnson, Peter. Johnson is the name on the mailbox from the person here before me. The landlord never changed it. I asked him not to, and I pay my rent in cash."

"Why would you do that, Paul?"

"Oh Peter, I'm a weak man, weak flesh, weak mind. I've gotten myself into a situation now where I want to remain anonymous, and I need to leave."

"What could you have possibly done?"

"I have a sad addiction, Peter. We all have our forbidden fruit, you know, the things that drive us mad with desire."

"We are human," Charlie agreed.

"That's a good way to put it," Paul said.

"And man cannot live by bread alone," Charlie added.

Paul nodded vigorously. "I think you understand me, Peter."

"I understand me, Paul," Charlie said. "I know my demons. You can't know anyone else until you know yourself, like you can't let yourself be loved until you know how to love."

Charlie was running out of Christian clichés.

"These things are true."

"What have you done, Paul?"

"I can't bear to hear myself even say it."

"Have you sought absolution? Have you confessed your sins?"

"I can't, Peter. I can't shoulder the penance. The remainder of my life will be my prison, my hell. Besides, no one can grant absolution for this sin. I would end up in a cell, and I'm too weak for a cell. Those dogs would eat me alive."

"Its your choice, Paul," Charlie said.

"Peter, I killed a girl."

"Jesus," Charlie gasped.

"She was homeless," he went on, "she was beautiful. Her eyes, Peter, they were so clear, so perfect. They were such a blue they appeared gray."

"What," Charlie said, but Paul was in the trance of his story and did not hear.

"She approached my van as I pulled in for the night, at my previous apartment," Paul went on. "She asked for money. I gave her a miniature New Testament. We started to speak of the

Lord. It began to snow. We sought the shelter of the doorway. The light from the street lamps made her look like an angel, with her wisps of blond hair peeking out from underneath her stocking cap.

"Paul," Charlie snapped.

But he went on.

"Her nose was running. We came upstairs. She said she would do anything I wanted for money. I gave her all I had. It was only thirty dollars. I told her I wanted nothing. She began to cry. She asked if I could get more. I told her I could in the morning. I moved beside her, to comfort her. I hugged her, our eyes caught, and they took hold on me. It was like I was unconscious. It was as though my soul drifted above my body and hovered there. Peter, I saw myself lose control. I saw the rage of Satan take hold of my body and I watched myself as I pinned her down, kissing her wildly. I watched myself strip her bare. There was nothing I could do to stop it. She fought me hard, but I was too strong. She wore herself out, and then I made love to her.

"She was crying, and by the grace of God I gained control of myself. She confessed to me that she was a virgin, and bathed in my own shame I did the only thing I knew I could do to vanquish the devil. I killed her, Peter. I strangled the life from her. I put her in a garbage bag."

And Paul began to cry. His head fell into his arms and he dropped to the floor onto his knees. He reached underneath the couch and grabbed the hat Charlie had given away in the snow.

"It still smells like how I remember her," Paul said. "I don't even know her name."

Charlie rose to his feet and snatched away the hat as Paul brought it to his face.

"You're right, Peter," Paul said. "I shouldn't torture myself with it any longer."

Paul grabbed hold of Charlie's leg. "I'm so weak, Peter," he said.

Charlie turned cold, ready to set the world ablaze.

He was preparing himself to kill.

"Peter," Paul said, "I can't sell you that van. It's yours. It belongs to you. Please take these keys from me and leave. Take the van and spread the Word."

Charlie raised his arm, ready to deliver the first blow.

Paul was sobbing and snorting. He looked up at Charlie. Snot was all over his face.

Charlie was suddenly confused by pity, rage and absolute repulsion, both of this man and of himself.

His arm dropped back down to his side. He left the keys in Paul's fat, trembling hand, and left the van where it was parked. He didn't want anything to do with it.

He put on his old hat and walked home, arriving too late to join Mother for dinner.

Charlie went straight to his room, and to bed, after locking the door as Sajak had asked him to do.

CHAPTER 16

Momentum mixed with anger makes rage.
Mrs. Bernstein knows a little something about that, rage, not Momentum.

She also knows a little something about hate, deceit, lust, greed, regret and guilt.

Mr. Bernstein was not at home, so we'll leave him out of it, but he knows an awful lot of things as well.

But he was not home, and this was unusual.

Charlie commented on this as he climbed the stairs to the bedroom as Mrs. Bernstein had ordered.

SD ALLISON

"Where's Mr. Bernstein," is what he said.

"Not here," is what she replied.

And they were soon without clothes.

So they did then what they always did, but something was different. It was Charlie.

He was not pretending at the moment, he was just fucking, and he was racing like mad to get done. Charlie stayed on top of her, ignoring her cues to roll over, grabbing and squeezing her tits, throwing himself into her again and again.

Charlie had her squeaking and moaning, squirming in constant orgasm.

Her dentures fell out, onto the floor.

Charlie himself was letting the presence of his enjoyment known.

"Yes, Charlie," she screamed. "Yes!"

Getting close, he started to let go, past the point he'd learned to stop at.

"Wait," she said, and Charlie kept going, getting very, very close. "Wait," she said again, "Charlie, wait."

"What," Charlie said sharply, and out of breath.

"Finish inside me," she said.

"What?"

"Cum in me."

"What? Why?"

"Because I want you to, because you never do. I'm giving you permission."

"I can't," he said, and stopped.

"Charlie, I'm not about to get pregnant."

"Jesus," Charlie said and pulled out of her.

"What the fuck is this," Mrs. Bernstein said like the bitch she was. "Put that thing back in me."

"No."

"No? Did you just tell me, no? I don't think so, Charlie." She scooched her hips toward him. "You finish the fucking job."

"No," Charlie said again and got off the bed, heading for the bathroom.

"I'll fire you," she threatened.

"Then fire me," he taunted back.

At this moment he had nothing to lose.

"Charlie," she called after him, "please."

"Why?" Charlie said frustrated and nude, not trying to hide himself, hanging stiff and slightly down to the left.

"Because I want you to. Because," she paused, "because this time was different. Because this time it was almost like I was feeling," and she thought a second, "like I was feeling *something*. I forgot what it's like. It's like I've been dead. I forgot how it feels to have that sort of life, that warmth inside of me. I need it Charlie. I don't like always feeling the way I do. I don't like this life we have, this mechanical fucking."

"Then we shouldn't do it anymore."

"It isn't that, Charlie. I like to get fucked by a young man. I like the way your body feels against mine, and inside of mine. I like how hard we fuck, like animals. That's not what it's about. It leaves me feeling empty."

"Well, I'm sorry."

"Listen, you little prick, don't you talk to me that way. Don't you forget who the fuck I am. I'm not one of these little sluts you bang."

"I'm sorry," Charlie said, "I didn't mean it to sound that way. I just, I can't give you what you're asking for."

"Well why in the hell not? What's wrong with you?"

"You really want to get into all that?" Charlie said. "Look, we're just done, okay. That's all there is to it."

And Charlie cleaned up in the bathroom, and went downstairs. He wasn't going to clean today. He was just going to leave.

On his way to the door a voice crept out of the darkened study.

"Did you enjoy my wife," is what it said.

And Charlie stopped in his tracks, instead of running, like he wanted to.

"Oh," Charlie said, and walked into the dead dark study. Rich, thick, deep red drapes were hanging heavy, blocking out the day. "Hello, sir, I didn't think you were home."

Mr. Bernstein was at his desk, a cigarette burning in an ashtray.

The smoke was rising straight up in the still air, like a string suspended from above.

"Where else would I be, Charlie?"

"I suppose I don't know."

"I suppose not. So, back to the order of my wife."

"I don't know what you mean, sir."

"Come on now, Charlie, don't play that game with me. You don't think you're the first we've had, do you? You don't think I know what's transpiring in all the corners of my home at all times? The bits may have grown dull, but the mind, the mind is always sharp. I'm not your dumb old, dead father after all."

"No," Charlie said, "You're not."

"Thank God, because you would have just fucked your mother."

"You're right," Charlie said. "I just fucked your wife. And I fucked her hard."

"Yes, Charlie, I already know this. Thank you for your honesty, after all these months."

"You know," Charlie said, "I think I've had about enough of this. I fuck your wife because you can't. I fuck her because you pay me. I don't fuck her because I want to, or like to. She's a fat old bitch, and I'm done with both of you."

"Well, well, our Charlie has become Charles, hasn't he, kitten?"

"Yes, he has," Mrs. Bernstein's voice slithered in from the hall. She entered the study and passed Charlie, running her finger gently across his shoulders, and stood behind Mr. Bernstein, sitting in his chair behind the desk, "he certainly has."

"It seems as though the boy without a father has become a man."

"I'll say," Mrs. Bernstein answered.

"It is astounding," Mr. Bernstein continued, "the progress you've made, the growth. Really, it's quite remarkable. I'm proud of myself, I'll admit. I'm proud of my Mrs. as well. When we found you, you didn't have the balls to buy a postage stamp."

"Fuck you," Charlie said, his chin trembling with a strange sort of rage that made him want to cry.

"Ah, yes," Mr. Bernstein laughed. "Back to the beginning. Do you enjoy fucking my wife?"

"No." Charlie said.

"That's funny," Mr. Bernstein said, and picked up a large remote sitting to his side. With the press of a button, bookcases on the far wall moved forward, then slid open to the sides, revealing eight small television screens encircling one larger. With the pressing of another button, Charlie was watching himself having sex with Mrs. Bernstein nine different times, on nine different screens, the screen in the center showing video no more than a few minutes old, "because you seem to be enjoying yourself just a bit, Charlie."

"Dear," Mrs. Bernstein said, "easy on the boy. I have a suspicion he's a faggot."

"I disagree," Mr. Bernstein said. "I think he's fallen in love with you, a kind of Oedipal complex perhaps.

"Possibly," Mrs. Bernstein said. "He is deranged."

Mr. Bernstein nodded, "Camera does add ten pounds, doesn't it dear?

"Yes, honey," Mrs. Bernstein said with slit little eyes, "Thank you for noticing."

"Well Charlie," Mr. Bernstein said. "Anything to add before you're officially fired."

"Yes," Charlie said, "fuck you."

"Bravo," Mr. Bernstein said. "Very original, very good. Now goodbye. Your cash is on the table in the foyer."

"Bye, bye, faggot," Mrs. Bernstein added.

Charlie was now unemployed. He was also very pissed off.

CHAPTER 17

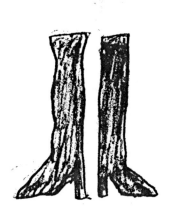

L ater that night Charlie was Jackson. Jackson, like Charlie, was also quite pissed off. He was with Cleveland and Monroe in their van.

Charlie was unemployed, but that didn't matter to Jackson.

Jackson was homeless. He didn't give any sort of fuck about it at all. He was too drunk to care about much of anything.

Monroe was complaining about the weather, and the nature of their chosen profession.

"I had a bad day too," Charlie said. "I got punched in the face. I asked for some change, and got punched in the jaw."

"This is what I'm talking about Jack," Cleveland said. "People hate us, fear us, and pity us. None respect us, but that'll change."

This was about all the business conducted for the evening.

Monroe said that a girl was coming by tonight. This got everyone a bit excited.

Alcohol and anger are quite an aphrodisiac.

They were all sixteen again, and giddy, like they knew they'd get hand jobs for sure.

Hand jobs are big around here, as is disappointment.

The boys were excited. They were looking for trouble.

She found them.

And after a while there came a knock on the van door. Behind the door stood Cherie, pronounced 'sha-ree'.

She was black, and attractive, if you could get past the fact that she was obviously a whore and that she said things like, "No, I ain't got no rubbers."

Charlie didn't know who she was, or how she knew Cleveland and Monroe, but he enjoyed watching her descent into a drunken sexual frenzy.

After a lot of cigarettes, and a bit of sleepiness, Charlie remembers her pulling down Cleveland's pants, and commenting on how much she loved white snake.

And things got a bit fuzzy here, because the next thing Charlie knew for sure was Cherie trying to pull down his pants, lipstick smeared all over her mouth. Her shirt and bra were off, and her breasts sagged lower than they should have, after years of having things put between them and squeezed.

She still had her jeans on, however. She said she was on the rag.

Charming.

Charlie was last in line for the night, Cleveland and Monroe were satisfied and tired.

Charlie wasn't sure what type of prostitute feasts on the homeless, but that was the type this girl was.

"Hey, hey, stop," Charlie said, and pushed the girl to the side, fastening his pants back to their full, upright position.

"Its okay, Jack," Monroe said, "this ones on me. You have yourself a good time."

"No, its okay," Charlie said, "I'm not, ah, I'm not really in the mood, you know?"

"Not in the mood," Monroe said. "What the fuck kind of mood do you need to be in to get your dick sucked?"

"A mood different than this one," Charlie said.

Cleveland sat back, in the back, watching, feeling the tension between the two build, but remained silent.

"Boy here's having a tough time getting hard," Cherie said.

"Shit," Monroe said, "I think you might be turning queer on us, Jack."

"Not wanting to get sucked off by a whore doesn't make me gay, Monroe."

Cherie then sprang to life, and a small blade sprang from her jeans, attached to her hand. It found a home pressed tightly against Charlie's throat.

Charlie didn't see it happen.

"I'm not a whore," she said. "I'm Cherie."

"Easy, easy, Cherie," Monroe said.

Charlie swallowed hard.

"I was just gonna do white boy here a favor and bust his nuts, let him feel on my titties, but I guess his cock is too good for a nigger to suck on. And who the fuck you calling, easy?"

"Nobody. Hey, Cherie, hey, this isn't a black thing," Monroe said.

"What the fuck does that mean, 'a black thing'?"

"Cherie, come on," Monroe pleaded, "you know what I mean."

"You know what," Cherie said, "I'm gonna cut this fuckers dick off, and then I'm gonna chop yours off too, mother fucker."

"Cherie, baby," Monroe said, "don't be like this. Please, honey, baby, no one's gonna hurt you. No ones calling you a whore."

"He just did," she screeched, tears welling up in her eyes.

"He didn't mean it," Monroe said. "Listen, hey, are you listening? We love you here. Everything's safe here. This is family."

"Yeah," Cherie said, "I'm sorry, baby. This is family."

And Cherie moved her free hand down and unbuttoned Charlie's pants again, and worked her way inside.

It was clear then to Charlie what kind of whore Cherie really was.

She was the really fucked-up kind.

"Yeah," Cherie said, "I think you changing your mind about me now, ain't you boy? Yeah, you liking this now."

Knife still in hand, and white snake in her mouth, Cherie bobbed up and down like she was late for some kind of appointment.

Here's some new slang: Beat Cabbage.

Example: That whore Cherie has one beat cabbage.

Cherie put down her knife then, to pull Charlie's pants further down, to really, as she said, "get up on in it."

That was when Charlie punched her in the face, and knocked her out.

Here's some old slang: Cold Cocked.

Example: That whore Cherie just got cold cocked.

This was the first time Charlie had hit anyone.

Today was a day of firsts for our friend, Charlie.

Cherie fell limp to the floor.

"Cherie!" Monroe yelled, and lunged for her, crumpled to Charlie's side. "Why the fuck did you hit her?"

"She had a knife to my throat!"

"She was giving you a blow job!"

"You're a tiger, Jackson," Cleveland said, breaking his silence, "a fucking tiger."

"This is so fucked up," Charlie said, and fought to open the rusty, driver side door, pushing with all his weight, and exploding out of the van when the thing broke free.

"I'm not going to forget this, Jackson," Monroe said.

Charlie threw back his extended middle finger to Monroe as he walked away.

Crazy people find this gesture offensive.

As most people are crazy, it's a very effective gesture.

CHAPTER 18

The phone rang in the middle of the afternoon the next day. It was one of those older-type telephones, the kind that still had a bell and hammer in it.

Nothing synthesized.

And that little hammer beat that bell like a rabbit scratching its ear, sending out waves from the kitchen that shook the oak floors and plaster walls in the rest of the apartment.

Charlie answered.

Agatha was on the far end of the line, just across town.

"Hello," she said, "I have an odd request of you."

Charlie was intrigued, and he found himself a few hours

later in a suit and at a wedding reception for a coworker of Agatha's.

Agatha didn't want to go, and wasn't going to, but making up an excuse on Monday and feeling like a shithead for being the only coworker who didn't show was not the way to start off a week, especially with this bitch in particular.

Nice that there are enough assholes and idiots to marry all the bitches.

So she called Charlie last minute, and now she watched him from across the banquet hall as he brought drinks back from the bar for them.

She was the only one from work who showed up.

On Charlie's way back to Agatha he bumped into the mother of the groom. She was around six feet tall and drunk as the Pope.

Let's pretend that means very drunk.

Physically, she resembled a rooster.

Charlie and Agatha got a little tipsy, didn't even talk to the bride, and almost danced once.

The DJ, 'DJ Jazzy Pat' was a real arrogant type of worthless. You know the kind, the kind that becomes a DJ.

And this MC with a goatee probably had sex with a bridesmaid later that night. Not that Charlie was jealous, not at all, it just seems to be the sad natural order of the world that no one seems to question.

Charlie and Agatha laughed about this as they sipped on their drinks on their way out into the lobby after DJ Jazzy Pat announced "no smoking" in response to Charlie lighting a cigarette.

The lobby was full of strangers with titles like: cousin, uncle, aunt, friend, and Rooster.

Rooster is a slang word for a woman who resembles a rooster.

"Well, hello there," she said.

"Hello," Charlie said, as a corpse would say.

"Hello," Agatha said, as a person who was alive but uninterested in the conversation.

"We've got to stop bumping into each other," The Rooster laughed, then snorted.

Charlie didn't say what came to mind, he just laughed like this, "Ha, ha, ha."

It sounded real.

"I don't usually drink," The Rooster said, "but tonight is my son's wedding."

"Yes," Agatha said, "congratulations."

It's sad when parents vomit at the weddings of their children.

"What do you two say to a little chicken dance?" The Rooster said.

"We're not really much into chicken dancing," Agatha said.

"But it's a wedding," the Rooster argued.

"You've got a point," Charlie said.

"I thought you'd see it my way," she said, shooting him with a finger pistol before heading for the DJ, "I'll see what I can do."

A minute later, as Agatha and Charlie were passing through the glass double doors that led to the parking lot the Rooster, and just about everyone else had begun to dance like chickens.

Culture.

Outside it was pouring down cold rain, thunder drowning out Charlie and Agatha's laughter.

The day had been warm, considering the time of year, but the north was mounting an offensive to remind everyone that she was still in control.

They laughed their way out, racing to the car in the rain. Shoes in Agatha's hand, Charlie flicked away his cigarette.

It was beaten by the rain and drowned in a puddle.

At the car, passenger side, fumbling to get keys out of a wet pocket, shivering, Charlie gave up and threw Agatha against the car. Tongues mixed with rain.

Keys jerked out of a ripped pocket and jammed into the door, Agatha fell in, Charlie with her. They fought their way into the back. Agatha undid Charlie's tie. Seams screamed as Agatha tore at Charlie's jacket. Charlie fumbled with wet buttons. Agatha slashed at them, tearing his shirt. Buttons hit the window. Agatha's fingers traced Charlie's thin stomach.

She moved and straddled him. Charlie's hands drifted between her legs. Hovering slightly above him, her thighs were tight, like smooth river stones.

Kissing hard and seeing stars, their teeth grinded as their lungs fought each other for air.

She lifted herself higher, and undid Charlie's belt. Charlie lifted himself to ease her struggling with his pants, and fought with her skirt and rain soaked panties. Agatha lowered gently, and Charlie was inside of her.

Fog on the mirrors, moving as one, Charlie was focused only on her. There was no one else in his head but them. There was no pretending. There was a future in the present.

They rocked back and forth, and front to back, rolling up and down, not forcing, not rough, simply moving together, like the rain falling in waves on the car and the earth.

CHAPTER 19

The circus was in town.

Charlie had only been once. He can't remember if he liked it or not. What he can remember are the two frog puppets his parents bought him. Their names were Francis and Fredrick. The shirts the frogs wore said so. Their tongues rolled out of their mouths when you triggered the croak, the 'rrrbitt'.

Charlie doesn't remember much more than that. His father died two days later.

Tragedy can help us to remember, or force us to forget.

Or, it can sometimes turn us into miserable people that no one wants to be around.

There are a lot of ways you can go.

Charlie was walking to the warehouse. He could see the lights from the arena illuminating the sky several blocks away.

Parking was expensive and tight. The garages and lots were full. The lines were long. Tickets weren't cheap, and people were getting their pockets picked.

Daddies always have cash in their wallets at the circus.

Charlie was stepping out of the Brotherhood tonight.

That was the plan.

Charlie thought about Agatha, and about Michael too. He should have been with them tonight.

Down the street a bit from the warehouse, the city was quiet and dark. Charlie should have seen a Brother or two by now. He should have seen Monroe for sure.

A section of newspaper tumbled end over end across the street behind him, and a rattlesnake shook its maraca somewhere inside of Charlie's head.

He realized then that he was alone, and quite a few blocks from something near safe.

Down another block at a businessman's pace, walking in the shadows, sticking close to buildings, and still no sign of life.

The warehouse was now in view, standing cold in the darkness. There were no geezers around a trash fire. The trash bin was a dead island in the middle of an icy sea of broken concrete.

The warehouse was a ghost ship. Spirits and demons danced as dust, lit by the moonlight seeping in through the gaps where windows once were. They escorted Charlie up the stairs, telling him of the mistakes they made and the women they once had.

"Hello?" Charlie said.

The scratch, snap, hiss of a match lighting answered him.

In the middle of the room, on the platform, Cleveland sat, sucking the life from a cigarette.

"Come on in, Jack." Cleveland said through the smoke.

"Cleveland?"

"Come on in, Jack."

"Where is everybody?" Charlie asked, walking down the aisle.

"Not here."

"Aren't we meeting tonight?"

"There's been a change of plans."

"A change of plans? So where is everybody?"

"They're at the circus."

"The circus?" Charlie laughs.

"Mm hmm. Hey, would you like to go to the circus? Would you like to go be like everyone else? You look like you need some fun."

"Not really, no. I want to talk to you for a second."

"Come on, Jack," Cleveland said and jumped up from the platform. "You need to get out. You need some excitement, some culture. You need the circus. The circus will be good for you."

"I want to talk to you Cleveland."

"They'll be plenty of time for talking later," Cleveland said and flicked his cigarette halfway across the room, heading for the stairwell.

Down, down and walking out the door, Charlie said,

"Is there some reason we're going to the circus?"

Cleveland smiled, patted Charlie on the back, and said, "Of course there is."

And if it were possible, the night had gotten darker. Clouds had moved in and masked the moon. Cleveland came up with two more cigarettes. Charlie was having a difficult time smoking the one he was given, trying to keep up with the pace Cleveland was setting.

"Why are we in such a rush," Charlie huffed.

"Because the show's already begun."

And another block raced away under their feet.

The auditorium now spread out before them. Charlie was sweating, and queasy from a thousand chemicals he sucked though fiberglass. The circus was on, and the line was gone, already inside and seated. The peoples were oohing and aahing, their faces sticky from pink cotton candy and their arteries wheezing from buttered popcorn.

Most of them will die from heart disease.

Physicians in the United States outnumber morticians 26 to 1.

Within a hundred years most everyone living on this plant today will be dead, especially you.

Charlie and Cleveland went in through the service docks. Cleveland nodded at the two oversized workers in overalls, waiting around for more nothing by the dock doors. The two gorillas nodded back.

Underneath the building, Cleveland and Charlie walked though tunnels big enough for a bus to tumble through sideways, if necessary. The sounds and excitement of the circus above echoed though the hall. Laughter and applause rolled for the champions of the freak show.

Through a set of huge double doors they moved, and on the other side Monroe stood, smiling sort of sick.

It's an empty storage room they were in, about half the size of a basketball court, with another set of huge double doors at the opposite end. Behind Monroe were two metal folding chairs sitting side by side in the middle of the room.

"Hello Jackson," Monroe said, sounding nothing like himself, sounding devious.

"What's all this?" Charlie asked.

"You'll see Jack," Cleveland said. "Monroe, have we selected our winners?"

"They're on their way," Monroe said.

"What's going on, Monroe?" Charlie said

"Patience," Cleveland said, and Monroe smiled.

Suddenly, screeching filled the world and the rumble of footsteps thundered close behind the doors at the far end of the room.

"What the hell's going on," Charlie said, and turned to see Cleveland now donning a handlebar mustache below his nose. He was decked in a coat with tails, leaning to the side on a shinny black cane with a top hat sitting crooked. Charlie staggered back, zooming out for the wide-screen. His face twisted ugly.

The doors opened, and the room was rushed by a hoard of twenty odd clowns.

"Come one, come all," Cleveland roared, "to the greatest show on earth!"

And all the clowns hollered, screeched, and flopped in delight. Inside the pack, a man and woman were carried along in the wave.

The man and woman looked quite respectable. They're what they're supposed to be, upstanding members of the American caste system.

The wife sports a grin as thick as those painted on the clowns. Casually correct, she could be sitting on a sailboat in a glossy catalog selling shoes, turtleneck sweaters and obsessive-compulsive behavior.

The husband wears a tired sort of confidence. His blood pressure has risen parallel to his stock portfolio, which consists of a healthy mix of international, large and mid-cap, growth, bonds, insurance, cash and tech.

He smiles at his wife, smiling gaily. She's so proud he's killing himself for her. He's so happy to be dying.

Behind them, a little girl no older than four, rides on the shoulders of a clown. She's twisted, looking back, smiling at two orangutans swaggering close behind. Their knuckles drag across the ground.

The orangutans are escorted by a muscley little person. He's the strong man of the circus. His name is Detroit. He's circus property.

'Midget' is like 'retard', in that we use a different word for it now.

"Welcome, mommy. Welcome, daddy," Cleveland said. "You two are in for *quite* a treat tonight," and the clowns all laughed a laugh that tickled the hair on Charlie's neck.

The orangutans clapped wildly above their heads.

Someone had mixed drinks for them earlier.

The little girl squealed in delight. Her mommy smiled bigger still. In her head she's crafting the story she'll tell her friends at lunch tomorrow about another perfect evening.

"Lets have mommy and daddy take a seat." Cleveland said, and two clowns escorted them to the chairs in the middle.

The doors the caravan entered through finally slammed shut, and locked hard.

Steel doors and concrete walls will keep the fun from getting out.

"Has everyone welcomed the real guest of honor?" Cleveland said. "Has everyone said hello to Jackson?"

"Hello, Jackson," all the clowns said in unison, and waved with hammed enthusiasm.

Charlie realized then that all the clowns were Brothers.

"What the fuck is this," Charlie said, just a breath above a whisper.

"Language, Jackson," Cleveland snapped, "we're in the presence of an angel." And Cleveland walked to the little girl, still on the shoulders of a Brother clown. "Aren't you a little angel?" He said softly, and reached for her.

The little girl leaned away, scared of the ringleader.

Mommy squeaked nervously.

"Easy Mommy," Cleveland turned and whispered. "Let's not make our angel tense." He turned back then and said sweetly to the little thing, "come here angel, its all right."

The Brother clown lowered her off his shoulders and handed her to Cleveland. He stood her on the ground, and squatted next to her, so they were face to face.

"Do you like Orangutans?" he asked.

She nodded shyly, yes.

"They're cute, aren't they?"

And she nodded yes again.

"You know," Cleveland continued, "if we could just get them to produce enough milk for human consumption we'd probably all live to be a hundred and ten."

And she nodded once more.

"So what's your name, little sweetie?" Cleveland said.

"Grace," she whispered.

"Oh," Cleveland sighed, "that's a perfect name for an angel."

Grace smiled at this, and lowered her little head like a little lamb.

"Tell me, Mommy," Cleveland said, "is Grace a smart little angel?"

"She's *very* smart," Mommy said.

And of course she is.

"I thought so." Cleveland said. "Tell me, Grace, do you see that man over there?" Cleveland points to Charlie. "Do you see that guy there? Jackson is his name. What do you think he is? I mean, what do you call someone who looks like that?

Grace shook her head, no.

"You don't know? Maybe you can't see him. Maybe he's too far away. Jackson," Cleveland said, "Jackson, come here. Our angel can't spy you over there."

Again, Mommy squeaked nervously. She already knew what Jackson was. She had no idea what Charlie was. She'd never even begun to imagine such a thing.

"Peace, Mommy," Cleveland said. "When angels learn to fear, angels become women, and we don't want that to happen, now do we?"

Charlie stepped across the room.

"Now, little lady," Cleveland continued. "Can you see him good now? Can you tell now what he is?"

And she nodded, yes.

"Good, what is he?"

"I don't know," she smiled, shaking her head.

"Let me give you some clues then. You see the way he's dressed, right? You see how dirty his clothes are? Do you notice how smelly he is? Stinky, stinky. That means that he's poor. Poor people always stink, don't they?"

Again, the angel nods.

"Do you know what you call a man like that now? Do you know what he is?"

Little Grace shakes her head no.

Charlie's face was still twisted an ugly contort of confusion. "Cleveland," he said, "what are you doing?"

"Relax, Jack," Cleveland said, "this is important."

"Okay," he continued to Grace, "I'll give you another hint. That guy, Jackson, he sleeps in a cardboard box, and asks people on the street for money. He's dumb, and he's lazy, he's a bit crazy, too. Do you know now what you call a person like that?"

"Grace," Mommy said.

"Goddamn it," Cleveland snapped, "no more interruptions!"

Grace exploded tears.

"Okay," Daddy stood up from his chair and said, very collected, "I think we're ready to leave now. Thank you again for the tour, but it is a weeknight. We really should be on our way."

Mommy stood up as well.

Suddenly, the clowns who sat them stepped in front and each pulled a pistol out of their enormous pants.

"Christ!" Daddy screamed, his voice cracking, and shot his hands up into the air. Mommy screeched and threw her hands over her face.

And all the clowns laughed and laughed.

"Those guns aren't real, Daddy," Cleveland said and smiled.

And the guns were obviously comical, having barrels on them a foot long.

Mommy and Daddy exhaled a lethal dose of carbon dioxide, and lowered their hands back down to their sides. Huffing and puffing, Daddy chuckled a bit, embarrassed slightly, seeing the clowns reenact his less than masculine response.

"Okay, okay," Daddy said, "you got us. But we really should be on our way."

Monroe walked over, in front of Mommy and Daddy, and pulled two knives from behind his back. The knives looked like steak knives, but slightly curved. He spun them in his hands like some sort of pirate and pointed them at the faces of Mommy and Daddy, inches from their noses.

"But those knives are real," Cleveland said, without a smile.

"So sit the fuck down," Monroe said, "and shut the fuck up."

"Jesus Christ, Monroe," Charlie said, "what the fuck are you doing?"

"Jack," Cleveland continued, "we're trying to find out how deep the plastic goes. This was your idea, remember, to find out what's beneath the plastic."

In the commotion, Daddy reached for his cell phone.

"What the fuck are you doing," Monroe snapped.

"He's calling the authorities, Monroe," Cleveland said. "Daddy is trying to call the police. Call them if you like, Daddy, but I believe you'll find it impossible to get service down here."

"Jackson," Cleveland went on, "the only way to see what people are made of is to force them to realize what they believe. You can find out the simple things they believe in the minds of their children. Children are easy to read. You ask them a question, and they'll tell you what they've heard, not what they think."

That's similar to most adults.

"Damn it," Daddy said, and showed the phone to Mommy, "no fucking service."

"Its okay, Daddy," Cleveland said. "The little angel gets her brains from you, no doubt."

"Can we please go," Mommy begged, tears streaming down her face.

"Can we please go," Monroe mocked, running the tips of the blades down his face, mirroring mommy's tears.

And the clowns all laughed like clowns.

"Really," Charlie said, "is this necessary? I mean, do we have to do it this way? Do we have to terrorize a family?"

"I don't see why not," Cleveland said.

"You don't see why not?"

"No, I don't, and I'll show you." Cleveland turned to Grace, still standing near. He touched Grace's jaw with his index finger, turning her head and attention back to him.

Mommy was sobbing hysterically in her hair.

"Angel, honey, do you know what this guy is? Do you know what Jackson here is? There's a big prize in it for you if you do."

And her face lights up as she exclaims, "He's a bum!"

The clowns cheered like it was New Year's Eve. Detroit escorted the Orangutans over to the little girl, and they handed her a little stuffed Orangutan, and each gave her a kiss on the cheek.

"Ahh," all the clowns sighed sweetly.

"And I'll bet you," Cleveland said, "I'll bet you a bullet in your fucking skull that she learned about all us dangerous, rotten bums from her gift wrapped little Mommy, and her little Daddy, too. How is this cycle ever going to end when we've got stupid, spoiled, rich mommies like that filling their sweet children's heads with filth?"

"Cleveland, what the fuck? This is fucking insane. We can't do this to people."

"Why not? They're doing it to us."

"No one's terrorizing our children in the basement at the circus."

"Jesus, it was a metaphor, Jackson."

"I know it was a fucking metaphor, Cleveland, I'm just saying..."

"Don't quit the movement you inspired."

"Cleveland, I didn't inspire any of this. This was all you."

"What's beneath the plastic, Jackson?"

"I don't care!"

"You don't care?"

"Not this much. Look, this is over, Cleveland. I'm done. I'm out."

"Well," Cleveland said, "that is disappointing."

"That's hardly the word I would use for it," Charlie said.

"Well, what is the word you would use?"

"Fucked up."

"That's two words, I think."

Cleveland had him there.

"Look, I'll keep this all a secret," Charlie said, "don't worry. I won't tell a soul. I'm just..."

"I'm not worried," Cleveland interrupted. "I know you're good at keeping secrets, Charlie."

And every drop of blood inside of Charlie froze.

"What did you just call me?" Charlie said.

"I don't know," Cleveland said, and turned to Monroe, "Did you hear me call him anything?"

Monroe shook his head, "I don't think so."

"Well, maybe it was the wind then," Cleveland said. "Maybe it was a noise that sounded like a word, like sometimes how when a cat purrs, or a dog barks it sounds like they're talking. Maybe it was something like that. I don't know. Or, maybe we know a little more about you than you think, Charlie."

Charlie backed toward the door.

"Are you leaving, Charlie, so soon?" Cleveland asked.

Charlie said nothing. He couldn't have if he wanted to.

Charlie was in shock.

"You can leave, we won't stop you. But you know what,"

Cleveland said, "we aren't letting you go for good. You don't just quit the Brotherhood. You don't just quit your family. That's what we are, like it or not. And besides, we're not done with you just yet. So, good night, Brother. We'll see you soon."

Charlie turned for the doors.

"Oh, and Charlie," Cleveland called. "You're running low on Tomato soup. You should pick some up. It's Mother's favorite, after all."

Charlie slowly turned back around.

"Don't touch her."

"What? We pretend to love Mother now? Charlie, why do we defend the people who hurt us? Why do we trust the people that cheat us? Why do we love the people who hate us?"

"My mother isn't hurting me. She's not cheating me, and she doesn't hate me."

"She's killing you, Charlie. Isn't that the reason for all of your other lives? Every second you aren't yourself is a second you're stealing from the life you don't want. It's a very clever thing you're doing, Charlie, but it's a dangerous game you're playing, with some very dangerous people."

And all the Brothers nodded, smiles creeping out beneath the expressions painted on their faces.

"A choice will have to be made," Cleveland continued. "What is it that you're living for? What is it that you're fighting against? What are you trying to achieve? I can't help you decide, but you must figure it out soon. Who are you, Charlie?"

And Charlie ran. It was the simplest thing he could have done. He turned and he ran.

"Don't be such a baby, Charlie," Cleveland called after him as the door slammed behind.

He ran through the belly of the arena, with the walls closing in, and out into the night with the icy moon glaring down.

Charlie's lungs burned cold on the frozen air.

Ice began falling from the sky. It pounded the earth and bounced off the cars, hopping along the street like maggots possessed.

Charlie was running. He was running to the only thing he had that was real, the only thing that he wanted to be real.

CHAPTER 20

Hands on his knees, huffing and puffing, his hair was an ice tray. The sweat on his face was making plans to freeze just as soon as the wind picked up.

He stood on the front steps of her apartment building and punched on the button next to the name 'Murff', bruising the buttons all around it.

His hands were frozen into fists.

"What?" a tired voice cracked out of the speaker.

"Agatha," Charlie huffed. "It's me, let me up."

"Charlie? Christ, its 2AM."

And leather-clad drunks falling out of The 69er confirmed this.

"I know," Charlie said, "It's important."

"It better be," she said.

"It is."

Charlie let go of the intercom.

He stood there for what seemed like minutes, exhausted and frozen, powered by fading adrenaline.

He was shaking. He couldn't feel anything. Bile crawled unnoticed up his throat.

Finally Agatha stepped from the elevator down the hall.

And this was it, he realized. The beans were about to be spilt. He was going to tell her everything, and why shouldn't he? Agatha would understand.

She opened the door and walked into the little entryway, which kept the inside from getting out, and she opened the security door, which kept the outside from getting in.

Already Agatha's tired body struggled for warmth beneath her pink fuzzy robe and the scarf she had thought to grab at the last second.

She was as beautiful as Charlie had ever seen her, so plain and simple.

Charlie was obviously delirious.

Still, he had never been attracted to someone on so many levels and in so many ways. He had never wanted to be with someone the way he wanted to be with her at this moment. He never wanted to be who he was until now. He wanted to be himself.

And then he opened his mouth.

I'm a housekeeper. I'm an adulterer. I'm a whore. I'm a dropout. I'm a liar. I'm retarded. I'm homeless. I live with my mother. I'm an anarchist. I'm an idiot. I'm a fraud. I'm a fake. I'm a Pretender. And, I'm in love with you, too.

This is what Charlie said, more or less.

"Goodbye, Charlie."

This is what Agatha said, exactly.

Then Charlie pleaded.

Agatha didn't say a word. She could feel the tears rushing silently down her cheeks. She could taste them, collecting in the corners of her mouth. She held her breath. She didn't blink. It was all she could do to stay together.

Charlie ran out of words, and Agatha retreated inside. She walked back to the elevator, crying. Half devastated, and equal quarters angry and ashamed, because she had fallen in love with another asshole.

By the time the elevator doors opened again Agatha had run out of tears. She was a mother, she told herself. She was raising a man. She had to move on.

Charlie was made of weaker stuff than that.

He let her go into the building, too exhausted to fight any harder to make her stay.

Charlie was breaking down.

He vomited on the stoop.

CHAPTER 21

Charlie no longer worked for the Bernstein's.

He sat on the end of his bed in his jeans, sweater and corduroy coat not ready, but willing to attempt his first day without Agatha, only out of the necessity to keep moving, and the knowledge that pretending was the only way to avoid pain.

And suddenly, Charlie remembered that he was in deep shit.

Our friend Charlie had just remembered the circus.

He stood up and whipped out of his coat, almost ripping off the sleeves. He couldn't breathe. The room was shrinking faster than he was.

He paced frantically, running into a chair, his desk, a bookcase. He started to take off his sweater, feeling it was too constricting, but stopped, realizing what he really wanted was a cigarette.

So he went over to the little desk of his youth, where he always kept a pack. He had a few left, maybe six, and they burned like a fuse.

He opened a window, and by the time all six were spent his room was as cold as a morgue.

He didn't leave the room that day.

He napped.

Fear is related to adrenaline. Both leave you exhausted.

Depression isn't related to either of those two. It doesn't leave.

It was dark when Charlie woke up. It was still winter, and now it was primetime, so he joined Mother exactly where he knew she'd be, exactly where he left her.

It hadn't always been this way.

It didn't have to be this way.

This is just the way it was.

Charlie sat down in his father's chair. It was old, brown and made of cow.

He hadn't sat in it really much before, just here and there, but never letting himself sink in. He was surprised how well it fit him, as it must have fit his father.

Mother noticed he had sat down and smiled at this interruption before struggling to catch up with the second of her world she missed.

The box flickered in front of Charlie, turning the room hues of blue, green and orange. Mesmerized by the flame and flash, Charlie's mind sunk into a chair of its own.

Doors opened on the screen, a half hour, or hour at a time. Each screen showed someone's life, or a group of someones' lives. They were sitting on couches at coffee shops, diners, or bars. They were in their apartments upstairs, or their houses down the road somewhere. They were attorneys, they worked in hospitals, and sometimes for the police. They were all funny, violent, stupid or annoying. Some people were gay, some just pretended to be. Each of these little broadcast lives were disassociated from each other, each unto themselves, completely separate, yet a part of something bigger.

They were a part of Mother.

Mother was a Pretender, too.

Days passed, and Charlie sunk. Television had begun to do for him almost what it had done for his mother, strip away the pieces of humanity, and blend everything into something resembling the waves and static from a channel not paid for. He was being swallowed by scripted, rehearsed, and embellished portrayals of reality, but none of it took away any of the pain.

CHAPTER 22

Weeks then passed in quiet, and in agony.
That was when Charlie began to drink.
In the liquor cabinet there were row after row of
the dusty old friends of his father. Mr.'s Beam, Morgan, Daniels,
and Cuervo stood side by side, their joints stiff, and their backs
aching, waiting silently for someone to come for them. And
one by one they were taken, spent, and returned as skeletons.

Mother didn't notice the exodus. She was so happy to have
her son again.

"Its good to take a break," she said. "You've been working
so hard."

Charlie had given up on sleeping. It was too hard to lay
silent in the dark. Thoughts crept beneath the door and scaled
the sheets of the bed and into Charlie's head. Charlie had never
felt as good in his life as he felt bad at these times.

Charlie had taken to passing out, drunk in his father's
chair beside his mother, the television lit like a Christmas tree
in front of them.

Mother was as happy as she had been in quite some time.

Charlie had abandoned his previous nighttime ritual and took up a new one of vomiting, then returning to his father's chair for a nightcap before passing out.

It wasn't cold anymore, at least, that's what Charlie had heard somewhere.

Waiting for a phone that never rings had turned Charlie into something real. He had become pathetic. Momentum was a thing of the past.

This was life.

This was a straight razor.

It was his fathers'. It was maybe thirty years old. It was dull.

It was just like Charlie.

Charlie had shrunk thin. His hipbones protruded, and threatened like a crocodile to engulf his torso. Eating wasn't something he could stomach anymore. Eating was only a means to avoid fainting.

He was like one of those patients who die while dying from something else, like all of us.

Charlie felt so tiny, naked in the dry bathtub.

He studied for a bit the calcium and lime stains surrounding the faucet. The off white patches in the porcelain tub resembled a huge decalcified tooth of some giant, depressed animal. He noticed the rust on the blade he was fingering, and the chalky scum swallowing all the green tiles around the old claw foot.

Neglect.

Mother was in the main room with her television lighting the way. Charlie felt bad about the scene she would eventually come to discover. It was enough to make him think twice.

In all the drunken time, between then and now, Charlie had considered the possibilities.

He had thought about going into the alley and climbing inside a few heavy-duty trash bags, tying himself inside of them. In the homemade body bag Charlie would bleed himself dry, and/or suffocate to death. It was a guaranteed way to die nice and good. He would tape a note to outside of the bag before getting in. This note would alert a passerby to contact the authorities, that a dead body was beneath the plastic.

This way, at least, his mother wouldn't discover him dead and the coroner could take him away safe and right.

He figured, however, that passersby would simply pass by, either not noticing or consciously choosing not to get involved. He would save his mother the horror of discovering her only son dead, but he'd most likely sit in the bag for a week rotting until some poor, curious kid who probably wouldn't be able to read the note anyway would take a peek inside the stinking trash bag.

Charlie didn't want that.

And now we understand why our hero is sitting naked in a dry bathtub.

Since his mother would probably die sooner than that illiterate kid it was quite likely, and slightly the lesser of the two evils. That, and he forgot he had used the last of the trash bags to take out the garbage a few days prior, so he really had little choice tonight.

A trip to the tub turned out to be the easier of the two evils.

Funny how life's little debates can sometimes end.

Speaking of debates. There's an ongoing debate raging in the suicide community, which oddly isn't a group politicians try to court, on which is better, slitting or slicing.

Both have their merits and faults. Slitting is exact, and while precise, it does go against the Bandage & Waxing

Theorem, which states that it is easiest to just rip the damn thing off.

Slicing on the other hand, while quick, lacks technique, which could leave you missing veins. Veins are the most important thing in this field. If you're not getting to the veins, then its just mutilation, and that's just plain wrong.

Charlie had decided on slicing.

And he sat naked in the tub, already having the reasons to the whys figured out. There were no rational chances left on which to back out.

His veins were thick blue in his arms, and spread every which way like rivers on a topographical map of some poor Southeast Asian country with an unstable government. He pumped his hands and flexed his arms. Blood began to fill those veins and push them closer to the surface.

Charlie closed his eyes and took a breath. He took a practice swing at his arm, then raised the blade one last time, and Mother came knocking on the bathroom door.

"Charlie," she said excitedly, "Charlie, are you just about done in there? There's something wrong with me. I think I'm getting diarrhea. I think maybe it was the clam chowder. I smell like rotting meat. Really Charlie, I'm in quite a state here."

"Yes, mother." Charlie said, and climbed out of the tub and crawled back into his clothes. He put the razor back where it belonged, and stepped out of the bathroom, and back into life.

He fell asleep later in front of the television.

As it turned out, Mother just had some bad gas. No big deal.

CHAPTER 23

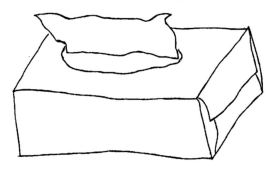

The day after a suicide attempt, or a failed attempt to attempt suicide can be a rough one. It's best to sleep as long as you can. Its also best to be around people you know well, but who have no idea what almost happened, or didn't almost happen, unless they are in some ways the reason for what almost happened, then that's not usually the best idea. Perhaps its best to stay away from everyone, unless being alone is the reason for the drama.

This is the sort of bullshit way of thinking that probably got you in the tub in the first place. So maybe just try not to think so much, okay.

Anyway, at least try to get some sleep. That'll help.

Charlie slept until noon, then made Mother her lunch.

Slitting, or slicing, again, this was the question? He sliced the grilled cheese diagonally, and slit a pickle down the middle.

After lunch Charlie sat on the toilet and read the paper for a while. Then he took a shower.

He took the shower immediately after departing the toilet, as is sometimes necessary.

Humans are a far from perfect design. Why we even grow hair there is anybody's guess.

He cleaned the birdcages, and then swept the floor.

"No school today?" Mother asked.

"No, Mother." Charlie said.

"Spring break?" she asked.

"Yes, Mother." Charlie said.

"That's nice."

And Charlie read more of the paper, until dinner.

It didn't take long before Charlie had rid the house of every drop of alcohol, but when he contemplated leaving to get more, he talked himself out of it. He was trapped, he felt. He could never again fit in his past life, and the life he wanted didn't want him.

Who are you when you're nobody?

No longer consumed by alcohol or Momentum, Charlie found the monotony of sobriety not as consuming as lazy people make it appear.

Our Charlie was no longer numb. Now he was feeling everything, and everything hurt.

One night he joined his mother in the TV room. He'd given up sleeping in the chair. He now chose to cry himself to sleep facedown in his twin bed, his feet dangling off the end. He couldn't sleep freely with his thoughts, and he couldn't turn them off. Pain pulsed from his chest and went rushing to all four corners of his body before rolling back again, ready for another wave.

"This is fun, isn't it?" Mother said, "You on break, spending time with me."

"Yes." Charlie said.

And Charlie's sad tone did something to Mother. The fog lifted for a second, and she looked at him, like she hadn't looked at anything in a long time, like she was conscious again. Her eyes were clear and alert, and she searched Charlie's face for something, but didn't find it.

"You're not happy, are you, Charlie?"

And Charlie's chin began to tremble. His eyes filled up, and his thin shoulders began to shake.

"Mom," he said weakly, "I don't think I've ever been happy." And his eyes let go, and the runoff of a thousand lies went spilling down his face. Shaking and sobbing, Charlie collapsed to the floor, and his head found a spot on his mother's lap.

But he was alone. The outpour of emotion was too much for Mother to handle and she slipped back into her world. It was happy there. Her late night friend with the big chin had just come back from a break to make her laugh again.

Charlie dropped down, and cried at his mother's feet until he fell asleep.

CHAPTER 24

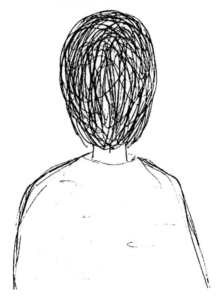

It was late that same night when the phone rang. Charlie had passed out a few hours earlier, half way through mother's visit with someone else.

It rang on for minutes. It didn't register in Mother's head what the noise was, entranced as she was by the picture box.

Mother has the focus of a wartime surgeon. You could say she was the Alan Alda of the convex end of the picture tube. You would sound stupid, but you are certainly welcome to do what you like with your life.

Charlie picked himself up off the floor and drug himself

into the kitchen. He answered the phone, and immediately regained consciousness.

It was Agatha.

"Charlie?" she said, and repeated it before he could even think to respond.

"Agatha, its me."

"Charlie," she said once again.

"Agatha," he almost shouted, "yeah, its me. What's wrong?"

"Charlie, there was a fire. We lost everything. The whole building went up. I don't think everyone got out."

"Is Michael okay? Did Michael get out?"

"Yeah, he's here with me. I need help, Charlie."

"Stay put," he said, and slammed the phone back on the wall.

He grabbed the car keys hanging from their hook on his way out of the kitchen. He flew through the family room, and past his mother on her couch so fast the TV Guide fell in a rainbow of pages from the coffee table to the floor.

"I'm taking the car, Mother," he said, and was out the door with his coat half on before she could respond, if she had chosen to listen.

The Buick started rough, and died as Charlie threw it into gear. Turning slow, and sounding sick, the engine did finally catch as Charlie gave it enough gas to drown a seal.

Charlie shot out of the garage and lost a hubcap in the process.

Sober, but driving drunk, Charlie ate up the road.

Miles away Charlie could see the smoke streaming up into the sky. Arriving, he saw the same thing, just closer up.

There were three fire trucks shooting streams of drinkable water at the building from below. Police officers were keeping the crowd of delirious tenants, drunk bikers and random gawkers at bay while paramedics attended the injured, as those were their assigned duties.

Charlie saw Agatha and Michael ahead, each holding on to blankets draped over their shoulders, just as a director would have instructed before the snap of the black and white marker.

"Agatha," Charlie said and rushed through the crowd toward her.

He expected her to run to him, so he could sweep her up in his arms and spin her around, but this didn't happen.

Charlie's imagination had been victimized by television.

"Hi, Charlie," she said in a distant sort of way that made him feel out of place, and unwelcome.

He looked over at Michael. "How are you, buddy?" He said.

Michael just shook his head and shrugged his shoulders.

"Ma'am," a fireman approaching said. "Excuse me, ma'am."

"Yes," she said.

"The detective would like to speak with you a second, if you're able."

"Yeah, sure" she said. "I'll be right back, Michael, stay with Charlie."

There was an awkward second or two following the second or two that Charlie spent watching Agatha walk away.

She looked even better than Charlie remembered.

Few things are more repulsive than someone ogling your mom.

Charlie had already asked Michael how he was, so he had to say something else, or at least he should have.

"How are you, Michael," he asked again, and received the same response. "Look," Charlie went on, "everything's going to be okay. Believe me."

Charlie had no idea how to talk to a child, let alone one whose home was burning down right in front of him, so he just stopped trying.

And they stood then in silence, watching the fire run out of things to eat.

"It's all gone," Michael eventually said. "Everything me and my mom got, it's all gone."

"It's just things," Charlie said. "It's just stuff. That's all."

"But it was *our* stuff."

"Yeah," Charlie agreed, and he had to, "it was."

"And now we got nothing, again."

And before Charlie could agree again, or say anything else that wouldn't help, Michael turned and headed toward the darkness, back through the crowd.

"Michael," Agatha said, coming back to Charlie. "Michael," she called again.

"Let him go," Charlie said, acting as though he had any idea what was right.

"Where's he going?" Agatha said.

"I don't know. I just think he needs to be alone for a little bit."

"How do you know what he needs?"

This wasn't turning out at all how Charlie had envisioned.

"I don't."

"Well, if you don't know then don't talk."

"Okay. Sorry."

"You should be fucking sorry."

"Agatha, did you call me here just so you could yell at me?"

"Jesus! Why don't you stop thinking about yourself for five minutes, Charlie. Not everything's about you."

"Fuck, I'm sorry. I came here to help. What do you want me to do?"

"I don't know. I had no one else to call."

"Well, you called me, and I came. If you want to yell at me, if that'll make you feel good, then go ahead."

"Fuck you, Charlie. I am so fucking pissed at you. You're a fucking liar, and an asshole. But I'm even more pissed at you because you're the only person in this fucking city I thought of that would help me."

"Well, then let me help you."

Agatha was exhausted. Her eyes were filling as her strength was fading.

Charlie moved closer. Despite the barrage of f-bombs, he wanted to hold her. Agatha backed away.

"The detective said it was arson." She said, stopping Charlie in his tracks.

"What?"

"He said it's too early to really know, but that's what it looks like."

"Jesus."

"I know. Then he's asking me if I have any enemies or anyone like that who might have done this."

"Do you?"

"Jesus, Charlie, what the fuck do you think?"

Charlie was thinking that Agatha was a bitch.

He decided to keep that to himself, however.

"Of course I don't," she continued, "but then he asked me if I was divorced, or estranged, whatever that is, so I had to tell them about Mike."

"You don't think he would have done anything like this, do you?"

"Not a chance. I mean, Mike isn't exactly a nice sort of man, or the kind that pays child support, but he would never do anything like this. Never."

Charlie then spotted Michael, and pointed him out to Agatha, standing toward the back of the crowd.

"He's not taking this well, is he Charlie?"

"I think he's taking this about as well as you could expect him to."

Again a fireman approached.

"Ma'am," he said. "We won't be asking anything more of you tonight, so you're free to go."

"Thanks."

He gave her a creepy sort of 'up and down' look then, "You have somewhere to go?" He said.

"Yeah," Agatha said. "Thanks."

Agatha was lying. The fireman had a mustache, and she knew that a woman should never trust a man with a mustache.

Charlie didn't catch on to the lie, but he did catch sight of the mustache.

The mustache thing is pretty widely known, or at least it should be.

"Where are you going to stay?" Charlie said.

"I don't know, Charlie. I hadn't thought about it until just now. I don't know what you're supposed to do when something like this happens. I guess we'll go to some Salvation Army or Red Cross sort of thing. I don't have any family within a hundred miles and I can't afford a hotel for more than a few nights, at least not the kind were I would take Michael."

"Well," Charlie said, and swallowed hard, "I know a place you can go."

CHAPTER 25

L ock the door, Charlie! Lock the door, Charlie!" Sajak
said.
"Yes Sajak, hello," Charlie said.

"That bird just talked," Michael said, a look of amazement
on his face.

"I didn't know you had a bird," Agatha said.

"I don't," Charlie said, and he heard the couch breath deep
from the other room.

"Charlie," Mother called, heading into the front room.

"Hello, Mother."

Mother's head snapped back in shock, and a smile exploded on her face.

"Well who do we have here?"

"This is my friend, Agatha, and her son, Michael. Agatha, Michael, this is my Mother."

"Well it's a pleasure to meet you," Mother said.

"It's a pleasure to meet you Mrs...."

"Oh, it's a great pleasure to meet you," Mother interrupted, and turned to Michael, "have you met my little Sajak?"

Michael shook his head no.

"Sajak," Mother said, "say hello to Michael."

"Hello, Michael," Sajak said. "Hello, Michael."

Michael smiled with every spare inch of his face.

"Lock the door, Charlie," Sajak said again.

"Yes, Sajak," Charlie said. "Hey, Mother, Agatha and Michael are going to need to stay here for a while. They had a fire in their building."

"Oh, that's wonderful," Mother said. "We have a guestroom. Did Charlie tell you that? I'll get you towels. Do we want coffee? Do you want waffles, or popcorn? I'll get you anything?"

"Mother, it's two in the morning." Charlie said.

"Thank you," Agatha said, "I think we're okay for now."

"Okay, okay," Mother said, glowing. "Michael, did you know that I have twenty-four more birds in the other room? I'll introduce you."

And she grabbed Michael by the hand, and they scuttled into the family room.

"Twenty-four?" Agatha said.

"Doesn't smell like it, does it?"

"No, I guess it doesn't."

"Yeah, my mom is," Charlie went searching for the right word, but was distracted by something he hadn't heard in years.

"There," he heard Mother say, "I couldn't hear you with that old television on."

Mother had turned it off.

"You're Mother's a riot," Agatha said, finishing Charlie's sentence.

"Yeah," Charlie said, not really comprehending anything that was happening.

He was thinking of a word more like 'certifiable'.

"Charlie, listen, thank you. Its nice of you to take us in."

"Its not a big deal. I'm sorry about everything, about all of it, I mean."

"Okay."

"Okay, what?"

"Okay, I heard you."

"Okay, I'm sorry."

"Charlie, you just said that. I know."

"Okay, well, just so you know."

He smiled then.

"Okay," Agatha said, "and just so you know, there's nothing that's going to happen between you and I. I appreciate you helping us, but I just can't trust you."

"I understand."

"Us staying here is only temporary, just a few days."

"I understand."

He wasn't smiling anymore.

Charlie's wounds were still too fresh to have something so blunt shoved into them.

"Charlie," Agatha said, "You look thin. Are you sick?"

"No," Charlie said. "I was drunk last month."

Mother returned with Michael, just as Sajak repeated, "I was drunk last month. I was drunk last month?"

And everyone laughed at this.

Even Charlie laughed a little.

It was as pleasant as anything on television.

CHAPTER 26

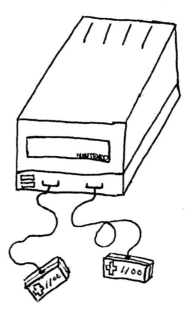

Agatha went to work and Michael to school. Mother began to clean, and bake. She had begun leaving the house again as well, usually just to go to the market.

She found that the real world really hadn't changed too much during her sabbatical.

People were still rude, and things still cost money.

Charlie sat around without much of an idea of what to do. When Michael got home from school, he had even less.

Charlie was sort of weird, and Michael sort of knew it.

Neither really knew how to talk to the other.

Luckily, Charlie found his old Nintendo, and a shoebox full of games, so they really didn't have to.

Together, Charlie remembered, and Michael discovered that there are few things more engrossing than video games.

Pornography can be pretty engrossing.

Mother wasn't watching much television anymore, so she didn't mind the monopolization of her TV.

The few days that Michael and Agatha were going to stay with Charlie and Mother had turned into a week, and then into two.

Mother made dinner every evening, and the foursome shared the meal together.

Life was a sitcom.

Here's further proof.

"Charlie's a bit of a loser these days," Mother said to Agatha in the kitchen after dinner one night.

Charlie and Michael were in the other room playing Nintendo, and overheard this.

"I think maybe he's taking a semester off school," Mother said.

"Really?" Agatha said.

"And he's so close to being done, too. So close to graduating."

"How far away is he?"

"You know," Mother paused, thinking, "I don't know."

"Well what's his degree going to be in? What's his field of study?"

"You know," Mother said, "I don't know that either."

That was when Agatha realized how little of a clue Mother had. It was also then that she realized how deep Charlie's secrecy went.

In a strange way, the fact that he had come clean to her, at least in the end, that he did let her into his guarded life made her realize the affection that he must feel for her, and the honor she was given by being the only person on the planet that he didn't want to lie to.

Oddly, it made her feel quite special.

When your apartment building burns down, your medications generally go down with it.

Michael paused the game, and turned to Charlie on the couch, "I don't think you're that big of a loser, Charlie." He said.

Charlie nodded.

Michael resumed his game, and Charlie picked up the newspaper sitting on the end table. He flipped to the want ads and discovered the shortage of accountants and sales professionals, and the lack of need for someone such as himself.

'Can pretend to be anything,' and 'willing to have sex with old ladies,' just aren't the sort of qualities most employers are looking for.

Scrolling further down the page, well into the dead-end section, Charlie came across an opportunity that was right up his alley, and just down the street.

The next morning Charlie applied for a part-time position at a pet store a short walk away. He knew an awful lot about birds after all.

A week later he was hired, and finally under the watchful eye of the Social Security Administration.

Charlie may have been a loser, but at least now he was a loser with a really bad paying job.

In Charlie's first month at the pet store he earned what the Bernstein's had paid him in a week, but at the pet store he was entitled to a 30% discount on all non-sale items.

The Bernstein's simply couldn't match this.

Charlie's first purchase was a thirty-gallon, fresh water fish tank and stand for Michael. His second purchase was a hand full of Mollies and aquascape items: pebbles, fake plants and what looked like a stone head in the Mayan tradition, made of plastic.

It was a few nights later when Charlie's bedroom door opened and Michael's head peaked in.

It was late, almost midnight, almost morning and Charlie was exhausted from a shift he worked till close.

"Charlie," Michael said. "Are you awake?"

"Just barely buddy, what's up?"

"The fish are trying to give each other piggy-back rides."

"Yeah, they like to do that." Charlie said.

It was far too late and dark to have a conversation with a little boy about aquatic sex.

"Yeah. Hey Charlie?"

"Yeah, they like to do that, Michael."

"No. I was going to say, well, never mind."

"No, what?"

"I was just going to say how like, you're the closest thing to a dad I've ever had, sort of. You know, because, I don't ever really get to see my real dad. And like the fish and Nintendo and that stupid stuff, he never did anything like that for me before."

"It's my pleasure," Charlie said. "I didn't really have a dad either, you know. He died."

"Yeah, I know," Michael said. "Sorry about that."

"Its okay."

"Okay," Michael agreed. "Well, night, Charlie."

"Goodnight, Michael."

Michael walked back to his room, and was sleeping in minutes.

Charlie lay awake smiling for hours wondering if this was what happiness felt like.

CHAPTER 27

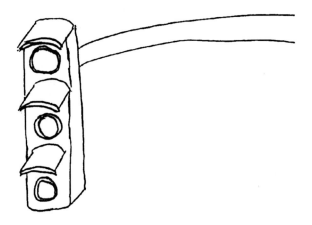

How much smoke is necessary to be labeled a plume is an intensely contested topic, but a column was rising high and thick over downtown.

The war had begun.

It was all over the television. You couldn't have missed it, unless your mother had turned it off to play cards with you, your sort of girlfriend and her son.

The game was Rummy. Boys vs. girls, and the stakes were low.

It was just a little something to pass the time.

This is an impossible chore if you're lonely and alone.

Charlie was not.

Agatha and Michael were leaving town in just a few hours. They were traveling to the Yankee Dakota to visit Michael's grandparents on a farm near a town that no one from anywhere had ever heard of before.

After the fire, Agatha thought it'd be good to try to reconnect with some family.

This is a pretty normal response to a semi-near near-death experience.

They'd be traveling by plane to Minneapolis where the old people would be waiting to take them the rest of the way in a Ford.

Old people like to put jam on just about everything.

Charlie was to take them to the airport, then claim them in 7 days.

Killing time had made them late. Mother sounded the gun and the three leapt from their chairs as though they were involved in some sort of game where the object was to leave your chair the fastest and get to the airport on time.

Traffic was not bad, but the lights were timed terribly.

Hit one damn light wrong and you hit them all.

People sometimes kill one another from such stimuli.

How Would Jesus Drive?

At any given second in any part of the world someone is driving like Charlie to get to the airport because they killed a little too much time instead of just leaving early.

We should each have our own plane and a runway. This would solve everything.

They weren't as late as they thought. They could have played another hand, but that would have made them late.

Life is full of these delicate balances.

Charlie walked them as deep into the airport as he was allowed, which was only about fifty feet these days. He and

Michael shook hands, just like how real people do, and Charlie plopped his hand on Michael's hair, tossing it here and there.

"Take care of your mom," he said.

Which was lame.

"I'll call you this week, Charlie," Agatha said, and quickly kissed him on the mouth.

Charlie wasn't ready. He wasn't expecting it at all. He didn't have time to pucker.

He kissed her again.

Charlie was the first man Michael had seen his mother kiss. Agatha had stopped being kissed by Michael's father by the time he was old enough to walk.

Michael didn't seem to mind. He just looked away.

Charlie waited, and watched them until they were out of sight. At the last second Michael turned and waved.

This made Charlie a little sad.

Sadness is sometimes a product of happiness.

Happiness is just a mixture of the right chemicals.

Science.

But let's not forget about the war.

Charlie turned to leave, but his eyes were drawn to the herd of travelers standing in packs looking up at the various televisions suspended all over the terminal.

He approached the nearest, as that was the most logical thing to do.

Wide-angled shots from atop buildings were balanced by zooms and sweeps, and finally back to the reporter standing to the side in the foreground. In the background, stretching deep, cars were lit and smoking, like Tiki torches from the Home Depot, or some other store with an endless parking lot.

The trail of burning cars led like the Champs Elysées to the park, where every tree, bush and blade of grass was burning. Even the lake in the middle, and the stream feeding it appeared to be on fire.

Awards would be won for this photojournalistic display.

"Terrorists," someone said to no one in particular.

"My God, not again," someone else said.

These two were a fair representation of the general sentiments and speculations percolating through the terminal.

A sharp 'shhh," followed every comment.

This can be a very disrupting sound if you're the one trying to talk.

"Authorities are not stating at this time what the cause of the blaze is," the reporter said, his hair made of wax, "and they are warning against speculation and asking for time while federal and local agencies investigate."

This was the first national broadcast by this local reporter. People who somehow knew him from his days in Oklahoma City, or some other city named after a state can't believe it's really him.

Someone behind a curtain in a room then switched from the reporter to shots of fire trucks with American flags flying smartly on top racing down wide streets, while military helicopters swooped down through the stone and glass canyons like the birds of prey they always seem to be named after. In the canopy above, fighter jets left angry trails in the sky searching for enemies they would never recognize.

The cameras caught it all.

If only Kennedy were alive again to be shot today, we might just catch a glimpse of Castro pulling the trigger.

In the distance the cameras zoomed in on a van not burning. The van appeared bigger and bigger on the screen until you and everybody else could read the words written on the side, in a sort of 80's shade of pink.

A quick cut back to the reporter, who wore a strange sort of glee on his face, not being able to mask his delight at what he believed to be irony and his chance to expel what he believed to be wit to a national audience, "and it appears as though that van was all that Jesus *did* save on this street tonight."

And the feed cut back to the national, where a more distinguished version of the same man from Oklahoma City, with hair also made of wax, agreed, and turned slightly to the side as another camera switched on.

It's always best to hear bad news from somebody's good side.

Charlie could barely stand up, but he was, and he was walking. He was the only one moving in the entire terminal and he wore the guilty look of nervousness as he made his way out of the airport, passing security guards and a German Shepherd on his way back to the parking garage.

Charlie could have been receiving a blowjob from a mime riding on the back of a hippo and left without incident. Even the dog's eyes were fixed on the television.

In the car now, Charlie was heading home at a snails pace, driving at the limit.

If everyone lived at the limit, like how they drive, the sanitariums would be full of really tired people.

If everyone walked how they drove, they'd wear out the seats of their pants from dragging their asses on the street, pulling themselves along by their heels.

Charlie was talking to himself now. He was telling himself to relax, that everything was all right. He was telling himself that he wasn't some sort of terrorist/anarchist, although he knew he was, at least part of him anyway, most of him wasn't, but not in any sort of sense that any court in the country would ever buy.

Charlie was slipping. A Pretender should be able to pretend that everything is fine. A Pretender should be able to drift from one thing to something else seamlessly. A Pretender wasn't supposed to be so nervous. A Pretender shouldn't be jumping at every set of headlights that pulls up behind him. But Charlie was no longer a Pretender. He was just a man that should have been watching the road in front of him, making damn sure he didn't plow through the police barricade ahead.

Charlie snapped out of it, and slammed on his brakes while an officer, standing in the middle of the road jumped to the side.

Charlie wouldn't have hit him, he stopped in time, but the officer couldn't see the event transpire before it did.

Almost getting hit by a car, or thinking you almost did, will piss anybody off, especially officers of the peace who resemble, and behave like gorillas.

There are certain types of apes who will kill their own children.

Humans, for instance.

Charlie jumped out of the car apologizing, but the officer charged him and tackled him anyway. In a second, Charlie was on his stomach, one of his arms jacked way up behind his back, and the headlights of the car that was behind now shining in his eyes. A thick forearm crashed into the side of his neck while his face was slammed into the street.

It all hurt very much.

"It was an accident," Charlie screamed as the officer put handcuffs on him, roughly patting him down while asking if Charlie had any needles or weapons on him.

Charlie answered in the negative, of course, and was then taken to a police station while the Buick was impounded.

Driving to the station Charlie was fed some scary crap about attempted motor vehicle homicide and driving under the influence.

Charlie was put in the drunk-tank for 45 minutes and given a sobriety test. In turn, he gave them a story about trying to get home to his unbalanced mother who was probably assuming the world had ended and had undoubtedly locked herself in the bathroom with a baseball bat to protect herself from the Russians, the Nazis and the Ku Klux Klan.

In the end they decided they didn't really give a shit, and charged him with speeding, although that was about the only thing that he was not guilty of.

Charlie signed up for a $75 class to be held later that month to keep it off his record.

Justice.

CHAPTER 28

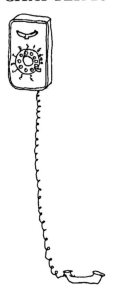

Putting his key into the door, finally home and exhausted, he could hear the phone ringing from the kitchen. Inside the apartment, in the darkness he fell over everything and tripped on a lot of nothing, disorientated by a place that is never usually dark, no matter what the time. There was no glow of the television, or the shape of Mother sleeping on the couch in front of it.

The phone was ringing, and Charlie knew it was Agatha.

"Charlie," she said, "I just found out about the terrorists. Are you okay? Is everything okay? We sat on the runway for about an hour before takeoff. We had no idea what was going on until we landed."

"Yeah," Charlie said, "I'm fine. How's Michael?"

"Oh, he's fine. It was his idea to call you. I mean, it was mine too, of course, but he said it before I did."

"Well," Charlie said, unable to keep the smile out of his voice, "tell him I'm okay."

"I will. Look, hey, we're at the baggage claim. I just wanted to make sure you were okay. I'll try to call you tomorrow or something."

"Okay. Bye, Agatha."

"Bye, Charlie."

"Hey," Charlie said, "tell Michael bye for me, too."

But Charlie was greeted by the dial tone. Agatha had already hung up. She didn't hear him, but Cleveland did.

"Very touching, Charlie," Cleveland said from behind, sitting in the breakfast nook.

"Jesus," Charlie screamed and spun around, dropping the phone.

Charlie flipped on the light.

"Fuck, Cleveland."

"Fuck Cleveland?" Monroe said, appearing out of the darkness behind Charlie, sending him leaping once again and gasping, "Jesus!"

"Who's fucking Cleveland?" Monroe said.

"How did you get in here," Charlie asked, but instead of waiting for an answer to that question, he asked a second. "Where's my mom?"

"That bird's fine," Cleveland said, pulling a laugh from Monroe.

"Where is she?"

"She's not important right now, Charlie" Cleveland said.

"I disagree," Charlie said.

"Noted. Moving on, how did you like the show tonight?"

"I think you've lost your fucking mind."

"Noted," Cleveland said again, "but that's not what I asked. I'll repeat myself, how did you like the show?"

"I thought it was disgusting and completely fucking unnecessary. Now where's my fucking mom?

"She's up my fucking ass," Cleveland said. "We're in the middle of a conversation I'd like to finish so I can get the fuck out of this aviary."

"Then lets fucking finish it," Charlie said.

"Oh, I plan to," Cleveland said.

"And what the fuck was tonight supposed to prove?" Charlie said.

"Prove?" Cleveland laughs. "Charlie, when did you get so stupid? This girl you're gaga for has made you soft. It wasn't supposed to prove anything."

"Then why fucking do it?"

"Charlie, you need people's attention if you're going to show them something. Tonight we got some attention."

"You destroyed a park, a beautiful fucking park. You destroyed a place that all of us enjoyed."

"So what? They'll rebuild it. One of the Fortune 5's will step in, get a tax break, some good press, and build a newer, nicer replacement, then we'll probably destroy that one too."

Monroe lets out a throaty laugh, still standing behind Charlie.

"Look Charlie," Cleveland continued, "its not about destruction, you know that. It's about opening eyes. Unfortunately, people are too numb to notice anything but destruction. We're just catering to our audience. Without the park the homeless will spill out all over downtown. The eyesore of our existence will be too much to bear."

"This is getting so fucking old, Cleveland."

"I know it is."

"Fucking stop it then. Class warfare has been going on since the fucking dawn of society, the dawn of man. It's not going to end. There will always be poverty. There will always be envy. There will always be homelessness. None of what your doing is going to accomplish anything. It doesn't make any sense."

"First of all, Charlie, you're stupid, and secondly, you're thinking about this all wrong. We're not trying to accomplish anything. We're not fighting to win. We're just plain old fighting. We're going to lose anyway. There's too much stacked against us."

"Cleveland, I'm calling the police."

"The police?" Cleveland said. "Charlie, you're not going to do anything, not unless you don't want to see your mother alive again."

"Where is my mom?"

"Monroe," Cleveland said.

Taking his cue, Monroe slammed a fist into the back of Charlie's head, dropping him instantly. Charlie crumpled to the floor unconscious, ripping off the door to the oven as he went.

CHAPTER 29

After a bit in the black, Charlie found himself coming to. He was bouncing around.

Charlie was in a van.

The van was moving forward, and rocking side to side. Monroe was beating Cherie's cabbage about two feet in front of Charlie. Ahead of them, Charlie could make out the back of Cleveland's head, driving.

Around Charlie there were wooden crates with a block writing on them that looked like Russian, backwards and hard-angled.

Cherie was moaning up a storm, and Monroe was snorting and grunting like a bull.

"Ah, Charlie," Cleveland said, seeing him coming to in the rear view mirror, "good morning."

Monroe looked over and smiled sick at Charlie, still giving Cherie the business.

"This is all just really fucking great." Charlie said, noticing that his hands were bound with tape behind his back.

"Monroe," Cleveland said, "are you just about done with her? I need to talk to Charlie."

Monroe's face twisted with repulsive concentration as he popped Cherie a few more times before pulling out, and shouting out, "Oh yeah, yeah, yeah!" shooting his little devils onto Cherie's stomach.

Monroe leaned back, sitting on his knees then, Cherie still twitching in front of him. "Yeah," he said, huffing, "I'm done."

"Good," Cleveland said, "come up here and drive. I need to talk to Charlie. And, lets drop off Cherie somewhere, okay."

Monroe slipped into the passenger seat of the van then executed the very delicate and clumsy transition of passenger becoming driver as the coach was in motion.

Cherie was fingering the jizzum on her stomach. She e looked over at Charlie. "Yeah," she said, "I remember you now. I ain't doing you no favors this time."

"I understand," Charlie said, hoping to God she meant it.

"Leave him alone, Cherie," Cleveland said, stepping over her, bent slightly at the waist. "Clean that shit up, will you. You smell like fucking eggs."

"Um," she said, "I love eggs."

Cleveland and Charlie both winced.

Monroe slowed the van, and pulled over.

Cherie slipped her shirt back on, and roughly pulled her pants on and up, still sitting down. She grabbed her coat and crawled into the passenger seat.

She and Monroe stuck their tongues in each other's mouths.

"You come see me later," she said, breaking away. She looked out the window and spotted a man walking past. "Hey baby," she said, stepping out, "you feel like having a party this morning."

She closed the door behind her and Monroe sped off.

"I'm really glad I got to meet her. Thanks." Charlie said.

"Don't thank me," Cleveland said. "She's Monroe's."

Monroe took a corner too fast, and Charlie's head slammed into a crate beside him.

"Take it easy," Cleveland shouted, "lets avoid getting pulled over if possible, okay."

Monroe didn't answer, but slowed down.

"I think he's still mad at you for punching her in the face," Cleveland whispered.

"That's understandable."

"Listen, Charlie, I don't have enough time for you anymore and have decided to let you off the hook. I just need you to do something for me first."

Monroe then took a slow turn and the road got rough. The van was bouncing and hopping. The crates shifted and Cleveland grabbed hold, trying to correct them.

The van stopped.

"Scootch up, huh Charlie," Cleveland said, stepping over him. Cleveland opened the back door of the van, filling it with light.

It was an early spring morning. Frost still clung here and there, but would be gone in an hour.

That was a passive aggressive form of foreshadowing.

"Throw your arms back here a bit," Cleveland said, and cut the tape from Charlie's wrists as he did. "I need you to help me carry one of these crates upstairs."

"Where are we," Charlie asked.

"At the warehouse."

Charlie awkwardly crawled out of the van. The drench of sunlight was beginning to make his head throb, his souvenir from Monroe's blow last night, and the beating he received from the officer.

Monroe had parked the van in back of the warehouse, adjacent to the wasteland of abandoned industrial sprawl.

Monroe turned out of the driver seat and hunkered through the van, helping Cleveland unload a crate.

"Help me out here, Charlie," Cleveland said as a crate was slid from the van.

Charlie grabbed Monroe's end and Monroe hopped out of the van, closing and locking the back.

"You go see to our guest, will you," Cleveland said to Monroe.

"My pleasure," Monroe said, and snickered at Charlie as he walked past.

Cleveland turned to have the ease of walking forward, giving Charlie the pleasure of walking the crate over uneven ground backwards and into the warehouse.

The crate was about three feet long and not all that deep. The weight was manageable for the two of them to carry without too much strain.

As they came around the van Charlie noticed written on the side, in a sort of 80's shade of pink: JESUS SAVES.

"Where did you get this van?" Charlie gasped.

"From the same sobbing fat man you went to get it from," Cleveland answered.

"You followed me there?"

"Charlie," Cleveland smiled, "I've been following you for weeks. Listen, we'll talk more inside. Your face looks fucking awful by the way."

In through the dock doors of the warehouse that Charlie hadn't noticed before they went and proceeded up the staircase.

The warehouse was empty, just a pigeon here and there, hopping about.

It was strange to see the warehouse in the daylight. It looked so sad and worn. Paint was peeling off the walls. The ceiling and floors wore cracks like the veins of an old woman's legs.

Charlie's lower back was beginning to ache. The lack of sleep, the numerous blows to the head, the sight of Cherie, and the strain of bending at the waist walking up stairs backwards was beginning to wear on him.

Charlie had been beaten more before 8AM than most people get beaten all day.

On the fifth floor, back against the far wall, there was a kind of trap door in the ceiling, the entry to an attic Charlie never knew existed. A few wood pallets served as a stool.

Standing on the pallets, Cleveland and Charlie pushed the crate up, and followed it through.

The attic looked like a kind of horror movie. Light came from bare bulbs hanging from the ceiling along a path of wood planks laid end to end, floating on a sea of pink insulation.

Where the floors below the attic were basically large, undivided rooms, the attic had divisions. The walls were made of cinderblock, and full of gaps and crumbling holes. It looked as though a sledgehammer had been taken to them. The lights dangling above played games with shadow and depth.

"Watch your step," Cleveland said, "or you'll wake up the fifth floor."

Cleveland took the lead now. Walking forward with his hands turned backwards to support the crate.

Making their way, slowly walking the planks Charlie nervously looked around and down the dark corridors that lay between rooms for as far as the light allowed. He was certain dead men sat at the ends, waiting to spring on anyone curious enough to explore the dark.

At this point in the story anything is possible.

Everyone could turn out to be albinos, or even Hispanic.

Zigzagging along the path, they eventually saw daylight ahead, streaming in from another door in the ceiling, leading to the roof.

When they came to it, Charlie looked up and saw Monroe looking down.

"Finally," Monroe said.

"Here it comes," Cleveland answered and he and Charlie boosted the crate up to him.

There was a sort of ladder attached to the framing that held this little opening they'd be passing though, and as Charlie climbed through he was greeted by the crisp morning, and his mother.

"Mom," Charlie gasped.

"Thank goodness," Mother said, "I've been up here all night."

"Are you all right?"

"Charlie, who are these men?"

"Nobody. Just people."

"We're his friends," Cleveland said, emerging from the hole in the attic. "We're Charlie's good friends."

"From school?" Mother asked.

"Yeah," Monroe smiled, "we're from Charlie's school."

"I don't believe you," Mother said.

"Mother," Charlie said, "please let me handle this."

"That's a good boy, Charlie," Cleveland said. "Watching out for Mother."

"Fuck you."

"Okay, Charlie." Cleveland said and motioned for Charlie to pick up the crate again, and they carried it over to the side of the building.

Monroe stayed behind with Mother, out of earshot.

The warehouse had a brick ledge at the top, all along the perimeter that stood a foot high. Cleveland and Charlie sat the crate down and Cleveland took a seat on this ledge.

Acrophobia is not something Cleveland suffers from.

Nor does he suffer from peccatiphobia or ballistophobia.

It'll be more fun if you just look these up on your own.

Cleveland grabbed a cigarette from the beaten pack in his pocket, offering Charlie one.

He also does not suffer from cancerphobia.

You shouldn't need to look that one up.

Charlie hesitated before he accepted. This was to be the first time Mother would see Charlie smoke.

Charlie didn't too much mind lying to his mother, but he did feel uncomfortable disappointing her.

At least, he thought, she didn't know about Mrs. Bernstein.

Charlie heard Mother sigh halfway across the roof as he lit up.

"It's a lovely morning," Cleveland said, taking a nice long drag.

"Let's just get this over with."

"Let's just relax, Charlie. Let's enjoy ourselves. This is a morning to be savored. Listen Charlie, whatever's gone down between us, and what's about to happen, I want you to know, I always liked you, honestly. You were the only one like me. You and I were the only ones not like them, like Monroe."

"How's that?" Charlie said.

"Well, for one thing," Cleveland breathed deep, "you and I aren't homeless. Now what do you say we open that crate?"

Cleveland bent down and began to pull on the top.

"You're not homeless?"

"A little help here, Charlie," Cleveland winced, the lid not quite ready to break free. "Well," Cleveland said as Charlie stooped down, "I've got a home, and a family, more or less, back in Kansas."

"Close to that homeless camp you found?"

"Oh," Cleveland laughed a bit, "I forgot I told you that. Yeah, there's no camp, Charlie."

"I guess I'm not surprised."

"You really fell for all this crap, didn't you?"

"Cleveland, I wonder how many truthful things we've actually said to each other."

"More than we realize, I'd bet," Cleveland said, as the lid of the crate came free.

Inside the crate was a metal box about the same size as the crate.

Imagine that.

After the manipulating of a few clasps, the box opened, and Charlie saw what contributed to his backache. It was a long shaft of a weapon with a shoulder harness.

Charlie had no idea what the thing was actually called, but in layman's terms, it was a rocket launcher.

"What the fuck is that?" Charlie said.

"Its what it looks like."

"What are you going to with it?"

"I'm going to make a ham sandwich. Charlie, I think it's pretty obvious. But it isn't going to be me who'll be doing it."

"So you want me to blow something up," Charlie sighed. "That's why I'm here. Well, that's just fucking great. And that's why my mom is here too, so I wouldn't have a choice."

"Well, that saves me some explaining, anyway."

"What am I blowing up?"

"The shelter."

"The homeless shelter?"

"Right again. Nice going, Charlie."

Behind the warehouse, across the mud and waste about a hundred yards away sat Saint Mary's homeless shelter.

"It's a straight shot," Cleveland said, "even your mom could hit it."

"Cleveland, no. I'm not going to kill homeless people."

"Better them than your mother," Cleveland said. "Those are you're choices."

"Cleveland, why this sudden change? First you love the homeless, and now you hate them?

"I've always hated them," Cleveland said, matter-of-factly, "Garfield getting damn near killed, LBJ getting jumped right in front of us, who do you think set all that up? Hell, we even got Van Buren a few nights back. He put three guys in the hospital, but they still got him. The problem was I couldn't get the right kind of people to help. None of them had anything to lose, so none of them really cared. I couldn't get enough good thugs to get rid of the homeless, and I couldn't get The

Brotherhood to start a revolution to get rid of themselves. The homeless really are lazy, Charlie. After the circus they all petered out. They thought the job was done. They didn't want to take it any further. And that's why I need you. You have something you don't want to lose."

"If you felt this way about everything why did you destroy the park? Why did you even bother with it if this was what you had planned?"

"Because I needed as many people as I could to go to the shelter. I needed to get them out of the park somehow."

"Cleveland, why the hell didn't you just blow up the warehouse some night during a meeting? It would have been a lot fucking easier."

"You know, I think you're right. Well, shit! Goddamn it! Oh well, hindsight's 20/20. We got to move on."

"You're a fucking lunatic."

"Yeah, yeah, yeah. We've been through that. Charlie, look, all you have to do is pull a simple trigger. I've taken care of everything. I've gotten you everything back that you lost. That's why I burned down your girlfriend's apartment."

"What?"

"Oh, you didn't figure that out already?"

"Cleveland, people could have died."

"Charlie, do you think I give a shit if people die or not. Look, no one did. Everything worked out. Everyone got what they wanted. I needed you and that girl back together. You wanted back together. I needed you to fall for that little kid. You did. I needed you to love your mother, and you do. You pull the fucking trigger, and you'll live happily ever after, I guarantee it. And, you'll never see me again."

"Well, that last part sounds good."

"I thought it might. I threw it in there for you."

"Thanks. Look, why don't you just do this thing yourself? Why don't you just blow up the shelter, like you burned down the apartment."

"Well, technically, Monroe burnt down your girlfriend's apartment. That was actually his idea. I'm not blowing up the shelter because I need you to have a little blood on your hands. It's an insurance policy. You can never rat on me, because you're the one who pulled the trigger. I won't go down without taking you with me. And now, with your having so much to lose, you'll never turn me in."

"Jesus."

"Genius? Thank you, Charlie."

"What about the guy at La Château, with the glasses," Charlie said, "he's in on all this too, isn't he? You got the weapons from him I assume?"

"Charlie, you'd be surprised how many people are comfortable with the idea of being terrorists, as long as they get to go home to their families at the end of the day. No, he's not involved. He doesn't really know who I am. He just knows a guy, who knows a guy, who knows a terrorist. So, are we going to do this or what? I'd rather not kill your mother."

"I'm really not sure what choice I have."

"That's the spirit!"

Cleveland picked up the weapon and gave it to Charlie, having him get down on one knee and into position.

"Just eye it there in your cross hairs," Cleveland said, "Point that thing and pull the trigger. Horseshoes and hand grenades."

Charlie was sweating. He began to tremble.

"You're doing this city a favor, Charlie. It's Sunday morning, all the bums are inside, eating their green eggs and government ham. One quick stroke and the homeless problem is no more."

Sweat dripped into Charlie's eyes. He looked down, and wiped it away. He saw the van, parked next to the building below. He looked back up at the shelter.

"Don't lose your nerve," Cleveland said. "Remember what's at stake."

And Charlie did remember.

In an instant, he lowered the weapon and fired, directly at the van. The rocket soaring down sounded like a match lighting. When it hit the van, it sounded like the world ending.

The van ripped itself to shreds as the explosives inside detonated each other, over and over again. The warehouse shook. The wall adjacent the van crumbled and fell in. The roof collapsed, with everyone attached, through the attic and down to the fifth floor, where it held, teetering.

Everything was coated in a cloud of asbestos and dust.

"Charlie," Mother cried out, "help me."

"Mom," Charlie yelled.

"Charlie, please help me."

Charlie began to crawl over the wreckage. Slowing inching toward his mother's voice.

Through the dust ahead Charlie could see Monroe standing above his mother, trapped under a slab of concrete.

Charlie arrived and stooped down, trying to lift the slab off his mother, but all it would do was wiggle.

"Monroe, help me." Charlie said.

Monroe didn't move.

"Monroe, the police are coming. If we want to get out we got to go now. We only have a minute or two."

"Its not my problem," Monroe said. "She's not my mother."

"Cleveland," Charlie shouted. "Cleveland, I need help."

The silence that followed confirmed for Charlie what he already knew. Cleveland was gone.

Cleveland never existed. Cleveland is only the name of a street downtown. As is Garfield, as is LBJ, as is Van Buren, and as is Jackson. That's just the way it is in the Brotherhood.

"Monroe, please. I need you to help. If they find us here, any one of us, we're done for. Cleveland's gone. He's left you. I need your help."

"I'm sorry," Monroe said quietly, walking away. "I'm sorry about the apartment."

"Monroe," Charlie shouted, "Monroe! Fucking bastard!"

Charlie looked down at his mother. His mother looked up at him. "Charlie," she said calmly, "get this thing off me."

Charlie again stooped down and began to lift. Charlie's face creased with agony as he strained beyond his limits. Mother's face looked the same as she struggled with all she had to assist. An inch revealed and Mother twisted free like a mouse. Charlie winced and dropped the slab, falling back, his hands gripping his stomach.

Mother was free, and in a hurry.

"Get up, Charlie," she commanded, and grabbed him by the arm, hoisting him into the air.

With his arm around her tiny shoulders, she guided them over the rubble to the rocket launcher. She dropped Charlie to the floor, and grabbed the weapon, wiping it down with her shirt as best she could, before covering it again with dust and debris.

"Fingerprints, Charlie," she said.

Not everything on television is completely worthless.

Mother grabbed Charlie again, and dragged him over to the to the stairs, which were shaky, but holding.

Bits of ceiling crumpled and fell all around them as they went, darting here and there like cockroaches. The building groaned like a dying elephant.

Out into the morning they emerged, bloodied, bruised and broken.

Two police cruisers were already on the scene, lights flashing, and an ambulance came screaming down the road. A crowd of on lookers had assembled across the street. Two officers approached.

"What's happened here," one of the officers demanded.

"We were out walking," Mother said, out of breath, "like usual, our Sunday morning stroll. It was such a beautiful morning, and all of a sudden the building just exploded."

"Why were you inside," the other officer said.

"We went inside to see if anyone was in there. The homeless live in there you know, we nearly got ourselves killed!"

"Did you see anyone, ma'am? Did they have beards? Turbans?"

"No officer, no one. You know," Mother began, "I bet this is some kind of insurance fraud. These property owner types, slum lords, I don't trust any of them further than I can throw..."

"Ma'am," the first officer cut in, "are you injured, you look pretty banged up."

"I'm sore," Mother said, "my ribs maybe."

"Young man here doesn't look too hot," the second officer said.

"Got a little over zealous, I'm afraid." Mother said. "He tried to move a beam, instead of just walking around it, like he's the Incredible Hulk."

"Got to watch that adrenaline son," the officer said. "That's a pretty senseless thing to do, running into a building like that."

"Yes sir," Charlie said, bent at the waist and dumbfounded by this woman he had never met but called Mother.

A paramedic rushed over then, a gurney folded down under one of his arms, another paramedic right on his tail.

"Let's have you take a seat here ma'am," he said.

"Now do I look like the one who needs to have a seat," Mother said. "My son can barely stand up."

"She said her ribs hurt," one of the officers said.

"Lets go to the ambulance and get you checked out," the other paramedic said. "Young man, lets get you lying down.

Charlie took a seat, and laid back on the gurney. The paramedics raised it and started for the ambulance, going over a checklist of injuries with Charlie.

Mother followed, an officer at her side, quizzing her, not quite suspicious.

"I wouldn't go in there," Mother said. "That place could fall apart at any second."

The officer collected contact information from Mother, before helping her into the ambulance.

"In the future," the officer said, "leave the hero stuff to the professionals."

"Well," mother responded, "if the professionals would have gotten here sooner, we wouldn't have had to do the hero stuff."

"We'll be talking to you, ma'am," the officer said, and slammed the ambulance door shut.

Later, at the hospital, both Charlie and his mother were questioned again before being discharged.

Mother had three broken ribs and a few lacerations.

Charlie had a few cuts and bruises, and a hernia.

They took a cab home. Charlie's arm was again around his mother's shoulder. Mother put her hand on top of Charlie's.

"Your hands are cold," she said.

"Yeah."

"Do you remember when you were little and we'd walk to the market in winter? Do you remember that I'd always want to hold your hands, because they were so warm?"

"I remember," Charlie said.

"God," Mother sighed. "That seems like so long ago."

"It wasn't that long ago."

"Your hands were so warm back then."

They rode the rest of the way in silence.

CHAPTER 30

fter a few days everything was back to normal, which it had never really been before. The apartment was put back together and the oven door was fixed.

The world had finally slipped through winter's fingers and all the real birds had come home, putting the pigeons back in their place.

Agatha and Michael had come back too.

The police had concluded that Charlie and Mother knew nothing, nothing about the warehouse and nothing about most things in general.

We all knew this by Chapter 2, but the cops around here have always been a bit slow.

Charlie had been promoted to Assistant Manager, and Agatha had received one of those insignificant corporate title changes, from 'Senior Teller' to 'Team Leader, Customer Care'. This didn't change the duties she preformed in any way, but it did earn her a 3% raise.

Charlie's promotion earned him another two dollars an hour, and gave him the responsibility of assisting the Manager with inventory and ordering.

The Manager was a fat white guy with a wispy red beard who played with Magic fantasy cards, and assumed everyone else was interested. Charlie had to continually think up polite excuses to get out of his weekly invitations to stay late and play with a few friends that would be stopping by. Luckily, it was soccer season for Michael, so the brainstorming of excuses wasn't too terribly taxing.

With considerable effort on Agatha's part, Michael was allowed by the district to transfer to the grade school close to the apartment. This was the same school Charlie had attended, until he went to Catholic School.

Agatha and Charlie had sex a few days after she and Michael got back home. It wasn't in a closet or a car. It was in Charlie's twin bed.

They didn't speak of the significance or insignificance of the act, nor the ramifications of it, they just held each other until Agatha decided she needed to take a shower.

This is always a good idea.

Michael and Mother were at the library when all this went down.

Michael and Mother were just about always together. She walked him to and from school almost everyday. They went to museums and the zoo. Mother even went to his parent-teacher conferences. She said she was his grandmother.

No one made a fuss.

Michael and Mother treated this originally as an inside joke. Eventually though, the joke caught the mainstream, and soon even Michael's friends referred to Mother as Grandma.

So, in a way, Mother's silly little dream had finally come true.

Just about everyone's had.

This is a lovely place to leave it.

The rest is very boring.

Born in Nebraska, SD Allison is the
descendant of farmers, teachers,
and men with bad lungs. He is married
to artist, Liza Otto, and is the father of
a little boy with autism.

For more information about autism,
please visit www.sdallison.com